IN THE
RANCHER'S ARMS

BY
KATHIE DeNOSKY

MILLS
BOON

Published in Great Britain 2013
by Mills & Boon, an imprint of Harlequin (UK) Limited,
Eton House, 18-24 Paradise Road, Richmond, Surrey TW9 1SR

© Kathie DeNosky 2013

ISBN: 978 0 263 90476 5
ebook ISBN: 978 1 472 00610 3

51-0613

Harlequin (UK) policy is to use papers that are natural, renewable and recyclable products and made from wood grown in sustainable forests. The logging and manufacturing processes conform to the legal environmental regulations of the country of origin.

Printed and bound in Spain
by Blackprint CPI, Barcelona

"I want you, Tori...

"I want to take you upstairs to my bed and spend the entire night getting to know you the way a husband knows his wife."

"I know it's probably too soon...but I want you, too," Tori said, sounding delightfully breathless. "But there's something I need to...tell you."

"What's that, honey?" Eli asked.

"I don't know what the protocol is for a situation like this, since I've never—"

"You've never made love before?" He wasn't sure he had heard her correctly.

"No, but that isn't—"

"You're a virgin?" Eli's heart stalled.

"Yes."

A surge of heat flowed throughout his body. Capturing her lips in a kiss that left them both gasping for breath, he pulled her up from the couch. Taking her by the hand, he started toward the stairs.

"We should probably discuss something first," she said, sounding a little hesitant.

"I don't want you to worry, honey," he said, kissing her when they reached the top of the stairs. "We have all night."

He kissed her again. "And if there's something else you think we need to talk about, it can wait until later. Right now, I'm going to make love to my wife."

Kathie DeNosky lives in her native southern Illinois on the land her family settled in 1839. She writes highly sensual stories with a generous amount of humor; her books have appeared on the *USA TODAY* bestseller list and received numerous awards, including two National Reader's Choice Awards. Kathie enjoys going to rodeos, traveling to research settings for her books and listening to country music. Readers may contact her by emailing kathie@kathiedenosky.com. They can also visit her website, www.kathiedenosky.com, or find her on Facebook, www.facebook.com/Kathie-DeNosky-Author/278166445536145.

This book is dedicated to my son Bryan
and his lovely wife, Nicole, who met online
and found their own happily-ever-after.

WANTED: Intelligent, well-educated, single female with high morals and good character, age 25–35, for immediate marriage to a Wyoming cattle rancher. Must have ranching experience, know how to ride a horse and want children. Only qualified applicants need apply. If interested, email: rancher_254@thehitchingpost.com

One

"Do you, Victoria Anderson, take Eli Laughlin to be your lawfully wedded husband, to have and to hold from this day forward, for better or for worse, for richer, for poorer, in sickness and in health?"

Reverend Watkins droned on, but Victoria couldn't have said whether the man recited the sacred words of the wedding vows or if he were trying to auction off a pile of manure. She was far too nervous to concentrate on anything but the ruggedly handsome, dark-haired stranger standing next to her—the very one whom she would pledge herself to within the next few seconds.

When the rotund little minister cleared his throat and gave her an expectant look, she swallowed the panic threatening to choke her. "I do," she murmured, her voice surprisingly steady, considering the state of her nerves.

The good reverend turned to her almost-husband and repeated his question, but Victoria heard none of the words. Two short hours ago, Eli Laughlin had been nothing more than a few long-distance phone calls and a half dozen or so email messages. In fact, during the course of their brief acquaintance, they hadn't even bothered to exchange pictures.

Not that it would have made a difference in her decision to marry him—it wouldn't have. There just weren't a lot of options for a down-on-her-luck heiress with less than five hundred dollars to her name and several death threats hanging over her head.

But she fervently wished they had at least discussed physical characteristics. It might have lessened her shock when Eli met her at the airport in Cheyenne. She wasn't sure how she had expected him to look, but she knew beyond a shadow of doubt, nothing could have prepared her for the reality of the man she had traveled over eighteen hundred miles to marry.

Of course, if she hadn't been so distracted by the hurried preparations and the urgent need to leave Charlotte, she might have taken a hint from the sound of his voice. She had always heard of someone having bedroom eyes, but Eli Laughlin had a bedroom voice. Smooth and deep, his voice could—as her nanny used to say—charm the bloomers off an old maid. The first time he had called to interview her, just the sound of it had caused goose bumps to shimmer up and down her arms and her pulse to flutter erratically. It stood to reason nature wouldn't have bestowed that kind of voice on a scrawny little wimp.

Victoria glanced up at him from beneath her lashes—

way up. When they had discussed their arrangement, she hadn't given his size a second thought, hadn't considered it would matter. She had been more concerned with convincing him that she met his list of qualifications, and listening to him outline his reasons for treating the marriage like a business agreement. But now?

The man was well over six feet tall, had the broadest shoulders she had ever seen and every time he moved, the most fascinating bulges pulled at the fabric of his chambray shirt. From her vantage point, he looked like a giant and a well muscled one at that.

Her gaze traveled to his face. Weren't men who spent the majority of their time outdoors supposed to have skin like leather? The only wrinkles Eli had were the faint creases fanning the corners of his dark brown eyes and the laugh lines bracketing his mouth.

"I do." The sound of him responding to the minister jolted her back to reality.

"By the power vested in me by the state of Wyoming, I pronounce you husband and wife," Reverend Watkins said cheerfully. "Son, you may kiss your bride now."

Surely Eli wasn't going to kiss her, she thought as she stared up at her new husband. They had met in person only a few hours ago when he'd picked her up at the airport in Cheyenne. Her pulse sped up when he put his arms around her and started to lower his head.

The feel of his firm lips when his mouth covered hers, and the sense of being completely surrounded by the man, sent a shiver of awareness up her spine. It wasn't a lingering kiss, more of a little peck really. But when he released her and took a step back, the brief contact had been enough to convince her that he was more man than she had known in all of her twenty-six years.

A moment of panic seized her. What on earth had she gotten herself into?

But remembering the prenuptial agreement, especially the part outlining a one-month "get acquainted" phase, she began to relax a bit. The marriage would remain in name only unless both parties agreed to waive the clause and consummate the union before the end of the specified four weeks.

"Congratulations to both of you," Blake Hartwell said, brushing Eli aside to hug her.

On the hour's drive from the airport to his attorney's office in Eagle Fork to sign the prenuptial agreement, Eli had explained that the wedding ceremony would take place at Blake's grandmother's house as soon as the document was signed. Eli and Blake had been best friends since they met in grade school. He and his grandmother, Jean Hartwell, would be their witnesses to the marriage.

As Blake wrapped her in a bear hug, she realized he was every bit as tall and muscular as her new husband. She briefly wondered if all the men in Wyoming were as large and intimidating as the two she had met thus far.

"Thank you," Victoria murmured as he turned her loose to shake Eli's hand.

Everything was happening so fast she felt overwhelmed by it all. Her first trip to Wyoming, the wedding and the fact that with a few quietly spoken words she had once again changed her surname were almost more than she could take in. It was surreal to think that in a little less than four months she had gone from being Victoria Bardwell to being Victoria Anderson and now Victoria Laughlin.

"Thanks for your help," Eli said as she abandoned her disturbing thoughts in favor of watching the exchange between him and his friend. "I appreciate you and Grandma Jean standing up with us on such short notice."

"Glad to do it," Blake said, grinning.

"I wouldn't have missed this for anything. It's not every day one of my boys gets hitched," Jean Hartwell said. Shouldering her grandson out of the way, she hugged Eli. "You treat this little girl right, you hear?" Turning to Victoria, she grinned. "You got a real good boy here. But if he does give you any trouble, just let me know. I'll straighten him out in two shakes of a lamb's tail."

"I'll remember that, Mrs. Hartwell," Victoria said, smiling. She wondered what the Hartwells thought of her and Eli's unorthodox marriage, but if they had any objections they kept their opinions to themselves. They had shown her nothing but kindness and made her feel as if their wedding was like any other marriage ceremony witnessed by close friends.

"You're married to one of my boys now," the woman said, kissing Victoria's cheek. "Call me Grandma Jean." Turning to the minister, she asked, "Would you like to join us for some refreshments, Preacher?"

"I'm afraid I won't be able to stay, Jean," the man said, smiling as he walked toward the front door. "I have to drive down to the hospital in Cheyenne to see a member of the congregation who came down with pneumonia."

After seeing Reverend Watkins out, Blake's grandmother motioned for them to follow her. "I've got a wedding cake and some of my best elderberry wine waiting for you two in the dining room. I know you'll want to get on the road before too long, so we'd better get to celebrating."

Eli watched his new wife follow Grandma Jean out of the room and wondered what the hell he had been thinking when he chose Victoria Anderson to be his wife. She wasn't anything like the woman he had been looking for when he placed his advertisement on the Hitching Post website. He had been looking for a woman who could help out with ranch work and eventually bear him a son to carry on the legacy of the Rusty Spur Ranch. But he would bet his next breath that his new wife had never worked a day in her life, much less on a ranch.

"You're the only son of a gun I know who could fall in a pile of manure and come out smelling like a rose." Blake's tone was low and quiet and Eli assumed his friend didn't want the women to hear him.

"What do you mean?" he asked, frowning.

"When you posted your ad on that rancher's dating website, you made it sound more like you were looking for a female hired hand instead of a wife," Blake said, laughing. "I wouldn't have given you a plugged nickel for your chances of finding any woman to take you up on an offer that sounded about as romantic as a trip to the dentist. But I'll be damned if you didn't end up with the prom queen!"

As his friend slapped him on the back and followed the women into the dining room, Eli had to admit that in the looks department, he had hit a home run when he chose Victoria. Her long, golden-brown hair complemented her lightly tanned complexion, and she had the most expressive violet eyes he had ever seen.

Unfortunately, beauty hadn't been one of his criteria for a suitable wife. He had wanted a woman who understood the daily operation of a ranch the size of the Rusty Spur and could pitch in to help if the need arose. And she had assured him she had the experience he had been looking for. But one look at his new wife's designer clothes and her delicate, perfectly manicured hands signing the marriage license, and he had known for certain that her claim to be knowledgeable of any kind of farm or ranch work was a total myth.

He had suspected as much the first time he called to interview her, but he chose her anyway over several other, more qualified respondents for one simple reason. Her soft Southern drawl caused his pulse to race. In hindsight, he probably should have been thinking with his head and not his hormones. But at the time, he had reasoned that if they were eventually going to have a child together it probably wouldn't hurt to find his wife desirable. What he hadn't anticipated was his reaction when he saw her for the first time.

He had always thought that having a woman rob a man of breath was just a line in a song or a novel. But that was the only way to describe what had happened to him when she stepped off the plane in Cheyenne. At first sight, he'd sucked in a sharp breath and he wasn't sure he had released it even yet.

"Eli Laughlin, stop standing there like a moon-eyed calf and get in here to help your bride cut the wedding cake," Grandma Jean said from the doorway of the dining room.

Grateful for a diversion from his disturbing thoughts, Eli smiled at the woman who was grandmother to all of her grandson's friends. "Yes, ma'am. On my way."

When he entered the room, Victoria was standing behind a three-tiered cake sitting on one end of the dining table. She looked like a deer caught in the headlights of an oncoming car.

Walking over to stand beside her, he tried to give her a reassuring smile. "Are you doing all right?"

She nodded. "It was very sweet of Mrs. Hartwell to go to all this trouble. I didn't expect a cake…." Pausing, she looked directly at him and laughed. "To tell you the truth, I really don't know what I expected."

Her nervous laughter and the vulnerability she couldn't quite hide caused an unexpected emotion to spread throughout his chest. For reasons he couldn't even begin to understand, Victoria Anderson-Laughlin brought out a protectiveness in him that Eli hadn't even known he possessed.

He told himself that it was because she was pretty, petite and delicately feminine—the type of woman who made a man feel like a man. But the fact was she was his wife and she carried his name now. For some reason that upped the ante. It was his job to protect her and it came as no small surprise how quickly the feeling had settled over him.

Eli took a deep breath. He must be losing it. Hell, they hadn't been married more than ten minutes and he was already thinking like a husband?

Emotions like that were something he had tried to avoid and approaching their marriage as a business deal, he thought he had done that. Apparently, he had underestimated the sense of responsibility that came along with having a wife.

"Okay, you two. Give me a big smile," Blake said, holding up a digital camera. He motioned toward Victoria. "Put your arms around your wife, dude. This is your official wedding photo."

If Eli could have reached over the cake to choke his best friend, he would have. Blake knew that he and Victoria were little more than strangers. But being thrown in jail on his wedding day for throttling the best man probably wasn't a good idea, Eli decided as he put his arms around her. He would just have to settle the score with Blake later.

When he pulled her to him, Victoria placed her hand on his chest and the warmth of her palm through his shirt felt damned good. Maybe too good. The prenuptial agreement they signed had a clause that stated they would refrain from having sex for a period of four weeks in order to get to know each other and find out if they were compatible. He took a deep breath. If the magnetic pull between them was as strong as he was beginning to suspect, he was in for a miserable month of bone-chilling showers and a hell of a lot of frustration.

The camera flashed and just as Eli was about to release her, Blake grinned. "Now give your bride a kiss. I missed getting a picture of it during the ceremony."

Eli wasn't entirely certain all the pictures were a good idea. What if, after their month of getting to know each other, they decided they weren't a good match and the marriage was annulled?

"Oh, yes, you'll want a picture of your wedding kiss," Grandma Jean chimed in.

Gazing down at the woman in his arms, Eli could read every emotion in the crystalline depths of her violet eyes. Victoria was as surprised this time as she had been when the minister told him he could kiss her after pronouncing them husband and wife. She hadn't expected him to observe the ritual then, and truth to tell, he hadn't intended to. But something about the way she had looked at him throughout the brief ceremony had compelled him to stick to tradition. The way she was gazing up at him now was having the same effect.

Without giving it a second thought, Eli lowered his head to cover her mouth with his. He told himself he was kissing Victoria because refusing would have created an awkward situation. Deep down, he knew better. He wanted to kiss her again, needed to see if his first impression had been correct.

The moment their lips met, he knew for certain that his assessment of the brief kiss they'd shared following their vows had been right on the money. Victoria had the softest, sweetest lips he'd ever had the privilege to kiss. The thought of what they'd do if things worked out between them sent his temperature soaring.

When his body began to tighten, Eli quickly broke the contact and took a step back. To his satisfaction, his bride looked as dazed by this kiss as she had the first one. Unless he missed his guess, she was feeling the same chemistry between them that he was.

"Perfect," Blake said, grinning like the damned Cheshire cat. "One more of you two cutting the cake and I'll be done for now."

"What do you mean, 'for now'?" Eli asked, scowling. Blake had been his best friend for as long as he could remember, but the man was pushing the limits of his patience.

Blake's grin widened as he rocked back on his heels. "I'll have to get at least one picture of Grandma throwing rice at the two of you and then another of you and your beautiful bride driving away to start your new life together on the Rusty Spur."

Eli ground his back teeth. Blake was having way too much fun at his expense.

After they cut the white cake with little pink flowers on it, fed each other a bite and toasted with a glass of Grandma Jean's homemade wine, Eli checked his watch. "Thanks for everything, but I think it's time we get on the road. We have a two-hour drive to get to the ranch, and Buck will pitch a fit if he has to reheat supper."

"You tell that old goat the next time he comes into town I have a bone to pick with him about refusing to be here for this," Grandma Jean said as she put on her coat and walked out the door. Her disapproval was evident in her stern expression. "He should have been here to see you tie the knot, and I'm going to tell him so." She turned suddenly and held up her hand. "Wait until Blake gets ready with the camera before you start down the porch steps. And be careful. He shoveled most of the snow off the walk, but there's still a couple of slick spots."

"Thanks for the warning." When Grandma Jean walked out of the house, Eli helped Victoria into her coat, then shrugged into his. "I had Blake go out a little earlier to start my truck and turn on the heater. It should be warm inside the cab now."

"That was thoughtful of you." Her smile sent a wave of heat spreading through his chest that he did his best to ignore. "And thank you for introducing me to your friends. I've really enjoyed meeting them. They're very nice."

"Well, Grandma Jean is, anyway," Eli said, jamming his wide-brimmed Resistol onto his head.

"How often do you get to see them?" she asked.

"I make it down here several times in the spring and summer, but after it starts snowing in late fall, I usually don't see them until the next spring," he said as they walked out onto the front porch. "My dad and Blake's dad were best friends and when I was young. I used to stay with them during the winter months so I could go to school." When he caught sight of his truck, he stopped short. "Son of a…"

Blake had apparently decided to do a little decorating when he went out to start the engine. *Just Married* had been scrawled across the back glass with white shoe polish, and a big white paper bell had been attached to the tailgate.

"I see you've been busy," Eli said. He cupped Victoria's elbow with his hand and they descended the steps.

"I take the job of being best man very seriously," Blake said, laughing. He clicked off several pictures as his grandmother threw handfuls of rice at them. "Part of that job is to decorate the groom's wheels."

"I'll get you for doing all of this," Eli said under his breath as Grandma Jean stopped throwing rice to hug Victoria.

Blake laughed like a damned hyena. "I never doubted for a minute that you wouldn't, dude."

When they reached the truck, Eli opened the passenger door for his new wife, but instead of helping her step up onto the running board to climb into the cab, he swung her up into his arms. She brought her arms up automatically to encircle his neck and he found himself surrounded by the light scent of her enticing perfume.

"Wh-why did you do that?" she asked, wide-eyed and sounding a little breathless.

"There's a patch of ice where you were about to step and I didn't want you to fall," he said as he set her down on the front seat.

She frowned. "I don't remember it being there when we arrived."

He shook his head. "It wasn't." Shutting the door, he turned and narrowed his eyes on Blake. "You thought of putting some water on the running board when you decorated my truck?"

Blake's unrepentant grin had Eli questioning his choice of best friends. "Yup. I had to figure out some way to get a picture of you picking up your bride, since I won't be there to get a shot of you carrying her across the threshold."

"What if I hadn't seen the ice and Victoria fell?" Eli asked through clenched teeth.

"Hey, dude, I know you better than you know yourself." Blake shrugged. "Living out there in no-man's-land, you have to be overly cautious. I knew you'd see the ice before you helped her into the truck."

"You had better hope I forget about all this before you find some little gal naive enough to marry your worthless hide," Eli warned. "Just remember, payback can be a real kick in the ass when you're on the receiving end."

"Since I have no intention of getting married, you're preaching to the choir, dude," Blake said, laughing. "You're going to have a long time to wait for your revenge."

"I'm a patient man," Eli said, waving as he walked around the truck. "See you in the spring."

When they stopped by the feed store at the edge of Eagle Fork for Eli to buy some supplies to feed a couple of "bucket babies," whatever they were, Victoria waited in the truck. So much had happened in the span of a few hours. From the time she stepped off the plane she'd been caught up in a whirlwind of activity. Now that things seemed to have quieted down and she had time to reflect, she wasn't sure she wanted to.

Staring down at her left hand, the simple gold band Eli had slid onto her finger during their wedding ceremony solidified her transition from life in the lap of luxury to her new role of being the wife of a hard-working rancher. But that didn't bother her. As far as she was concerned, money or the lack thereof was a minor wrinkle in the grand scheme of things. In fact, if she never rubbed elbows with the wealthy again, it would be all too soon. She had learned the hard way that when her bank account dwindled down to nothing, so did her friends.

But none of that mattered. What bothered her more than anything else was knowing she'd traded one loveless existence for another. Of course, legally they had a month to decide whether or not to stay married. But there was no guarantee, even if they chose to stay together, that they would fall in love.

She had hoped that one day she might meet someone who would truly love her unconditionally, but it didn't look as though that would happen now. In her desperation to leave Charlotte, she'd agreed to the businesslike terms of marrying Eli—a quick solution to her dilemma. And although it wasn't the fairy-tale beginning that she would have preferred for their relationship, she had every intention of trying to make their marriage work. She had given her word and that was something she tried never to break.

Sighing, she stared out the passenger window. Most people who were unlucky in love could take consolation in the love they received from their parents as a measure of their self-worth and importance. All she had to look back on was a barely tolerated existence by her father.

She gazed at the surrounding mountains as she swallowed around the huge lump clogging her throat. Her birth had taken her mother's life, and John Bardwell had never been able to forgive her. Now that he was gone, there was no chance of him ever forgiving her. Not that she thought that would have ever happened. She hadn't. But with his death, even the slightest possibility of that eventuality had been buried along with him.

Of course, she'd had her nanny—a woman her father paid to raise her. Nanny Marie had cared deeply for her. Victoria had no doubt about that. But it wasn't the same as a mother's love. To Marie Gentry, Victoria had represented a job and a way to escape the poverty she had grown up in.

"Is something wrong?" Eli asked as he got back into the truck.

Lost in thought, she hadn't noticed his return. "I'm just a little tired," she lied, shaking her head. "I think the time difference must be catching up with me."

"Why don't you put your head back and take a nap?" he suggested. "There's plenty of time. We have a two-hour drive to get to the Rusty Spur."

"I doubt I could sleep." She pointed to the mountains in front of them. "I don't want to miss this view. It's breathtaking."

He gave her an odd look. "You really mean that, don't you?"

"Of course." Nodding, she released a bit of the tension she had felt since her arrival. "I think it's beautiful here. I find the mountains absolutely fascinating and everything around me looks like it could be on a Christmas card."

"You don't think you'll mind all this snow?" His tone was conversational, but she could tell he had more than a little interest in her answer.

"Not at all." Smiling, she continued to gaze at the snow-covered landscape. "We rarely get snow in Charlotte and when we do, there isn't very much and it doesn't last more than a day or so."

"If you'll remember, I told you the Rusty Spur is in a pretty remote valley," he warned. "There are times in the winter that we get snowed in for a week or two at a time. You don't think you'll mind that?"

"Not as long as I can get out and build a snowman occasionally." Her smile faded. One of the things he had warned her about during their first phone conversation had been how isolated the ranch was and how much snow the area got during the winter months. "But we discussed this the first time you called to interview me. Didn't you believe me when I told you I wouldn't mind it?"

To her surprise, he reached over to cover her hand with his. "It's one thing to talk about what it would be like to be snowed in. You might feel differently about it when you're actually in that situation, Tori."

Her hand tingled from the contact and she could have sworn her heart skipped a beat. Deciding to ignore the excitement coursing through her from his touch, she focused on his shortening of her name. "No one has ever called me anything but Victoria," she said, thoughtfully.

"Do you mind me calling you Tori?" he asked. His smile increased the warmth spreading through her.

It seemed only fitting that she have a new name for her new life, even if it was just a variation of her given name. "I don't mind at all. In fact, I like it," she said decisively. "It's less formal."

His hand continuing to engulf hers and the feel of his calloused palm against her much smoother skin caused an interesting little flutter to begin deep in the pit of her stomach. She tried to ignore it, but it suddenly felt as if the spacious cab of the truck got quite a bit smaller.

"I know I won't mind the weather, but don't you

think it's a bit late for you to be second-guessing me?" she asked.

He seemed to consider her question a moment before he finally nodded. "I just want to be sure you know what you've signed on for."

She didn't want to tell him that no matter what she had gotten herself into, she hadn't had any other options. Nor did she feel ready to discuss her father and the disgrace the Bardwell name had suffered because of his poor decisions. She had even been forced to have her surname legally changed to Anderson—her mother's maiden name—when she started getting death threats.

If they were going to stay together, at some point she would have to tell Eli everything. But she had a month to find the right way to do that. And if they decided to go their separate ways, he would never need to know that for months she had been followed night and day by investigative reporters. He'd never need to understand the desperation that had driven her to marry a stranger or the guilt she would harbor for the rest of her life.

She took a deep breath. Watching your father cause the financial downfall of hundreds of his clients and lose his financial-consulting firm because of it wasn't something she was comfortable discussing with someone she barely knew. She had told him that her father died of a heart attack, but he didn't need to know that stress was the cause.

"Don't worry about me. If I wasn't certain of what I'm doing, I wouldn't be here." She covered a yawn with her hand. "Maybe I will try to sleep a little. Please wake me when we get close to the ranch. The way you described it when we spoke over the phone, I'd love for my first glimpse of the valley to be from the top of the ridge."

"I will," he said, giving her a smile that curled her toes inside her new fur-lined snow boots.

She wasn't entirely certain she was comfortable with feeling so attracted to her new husband so soon. It could be a plus if their marriage worked. It could spell heartache for her if it didn't.

When Tori closed her eyes and tried to relax, she decided it would be in her best interest not to dwell on that right now. She had other, more important concerns.

If and when she did tell Eli about her father and her part in the scandal, how would he react to learning that he had married the pariah of Charlotte society? Would he understand that in her desperation to get as far away from the shame and humiliation that she had been driven to search online for an area of the country where the Bardwell name wasn't as well-known?

Even though she held a master's degree in financial planning and had been cleared of any involvement in the illegal transactions conducted at the now-defunct Bardwell Investments Agency, no one in the financial industry would hire her. She just hoped that Eli could overlook the fact that she hadn't exactly been honest with him. And that he had married the daughter of the man who had helped to create the nation's biggest financial fiasco in recent history.

Two

When he stopped his truck at the top of the ridge overlooking his ranch, Eli glanced over at his new wife. Tori had fallen asleep almost as soon as she'd closed her eyes, but it hadn't been a restful nap. Several times during the past hour and a half, she had whimpered and murmured something. He hadn't been able to understand what she said, but whatever it was it must have been extremely upsetting. He had even considered waking her when a tear escaped the corner of her eye to run down her smooth cheek. But she had seemed to rest peacefully after that, so he had let her be.

As he continued to watch her sleep, he couldn't help but marvel at how alluring she was. He hadn't anticipated that, or the protectiveness that seemed to accompany the pronouncement by the good reverend that she was his wife. Both were feelings he had hoped to avoid.

He had thought by advertising for a bride, listing his specific requirements and making his choice from the qualified applicants, he would remove the possibility of any kind of romantic entanglement. He had learned the hard way that when an emotional attachment was involved, it clouded a man's judgment.

And truth to tell, after talking to her the first time, he had decided that she wasn't suitable, and moved on to interview other, more qualified women. But each time he ended a conversation with one of them, his thoughts kept straying back to his phone call to Tori. There had been something about her soft, Southern voice as she told him about her time on the family farm that compelled him to choose her, instead of using his head to select one of the more obvious candidates to be his bride.

Now he had a beautiful wife who he would bet everything he owned had no experience at all with livestock. What she did have were the softest lips he'd ever had the privilege to kiss, as well as a voice that set his pulse to racing each time he heard it.

"So much for keeping a romantic attraction out of the equation, genius," he muttered to himself.

Not at all comfortable with the direction his thoughts were taking, he decided to analyze his reaction to his new wife a bit later. He lightly touched her shoulder. "Tori, we're home."

Her long dark lashes fluttered once, then opened to reveal her extraordinary violet eyes. His lower body tightened as she gazed up at him. She looked soft, feminine and so damned desirable that he barely resisted the urge to release her seat belt and pull her into his arms.

"We're here already?" She sat up in the bucket seat. "How long was I asleep?"

"About an hour and a half." He forced a smile. "You wanted me to wake you when we got to the ridge above the ranch."

He heard her soft intake of breath and knew the moment she caught sight of the Rusty Spur Ranch in the valley below. He forgot all about his lapse of judgment as a sense of satisfaction filled him at the expression of awe on her pretty face. She was clearly impressed by the size of the operation.

"How big is your ranch?" she asked, her voice filled with amazement.

"You're looking at the ranch headquarters. There's about ten thousand acres here and another twenty thousand of pastureland outside of the valley. I also lease another fifteen thousand acres from the Bureau of Land Management." He pointed to the big log home his great-great-grandfather had built. "That's where we'll live, along with Buck. He tends to the house and cooks now that he's retired from ranch work."

"It's gorgeous and so big," she said, unbuckling the shoulder harness to sit forward for a better look out of the windshield. "I can't tell from this distance. What are all those buildings behind the house?"

Her almost childlike enthusiasm and questions caused his chest to swell with pride. The Laughlins had settled in the valley over a hundred and twenty five years ago and each generation had made the ranch bigger and better than the last.

He pointed toward the buildings directly behind the house. "Those are the barns. There's one for the work horses, one for storing grain and hay, another one for ranch trucks, tractors and other equipment. That one we use for treating sick and injured livestock and that big one is where we keep the tractor trailers we use for transporting cattle to market and to some of the far-thest pastures." Pointing to the far side of the valley, he added, "That smaller house over there is where the foreman and his wife live and the bigger one next to it is the bunkhouse where the single men stay."

"There'll be a woman I can talk to from time to time?" Tori asked, brightening even more.

"When she has time, you can. Sally Ann is usually pretty busy cooking for the men and she sometimes helps Buck take care of the ranch house when his ar-thritis is acting up." He grinned. "She and her husband, Jack, have lived on the ranch for as long as I can re-member. I'm sure she'll enjoy having another woman around after having to deal with men all these years."

"So she's a bit older?"

"I don't know exactly how old she is and I'm for damned sure not going to make the mistake of asking her," he said, laughing. "But if I had to venture a guess, I'd say she's somewhere in her early to mid-fifties."

Tori seemed to digest that a moment before she pointed to the corral and holding pens. "Are those..." She stopped, and he could tell she was searching for the right word. "...corrals?"

"There are a couple of corrals for the horses when we let them out of their stalls for some fresh air and ex-ercise, a round pen for breaking them to ride and about eight holding pens for the cattle," he explained. "We use those when we bring the heifers in from the pastures at calving time and to separate the stock during roundup."

As he watched Tori take in the vastness of his ranch, Eli couldn't help but marvel at the difference between her reaction and the first woman that he'd brought home to see the ranch. That had been ten years ago when he brought his college girlfriend home for Thanksgiving and it had turned out to be the beginning of the end of their relationship.

The woman had taken one look at the remote location and the amount of snow that was already on the ground and hadn't been able to get back to Los Angeles fast enough. She hadn't liked the stark beauty of the mountains, didn't like the smell of the pines surrounding the valley and couldn't believe anyone would want to live in something as primitive as a log home. Never mind that the house had all the latest conveniences, as well as satellite hookup to television and the internet. She hadn't even appreciated that at night the stars looked brighter and seemed almost close enough to touch. Or that there were so many they couldn't be counted. All she could do was complain about how dark it was at night and question why his father didn't consider selling off the land to a developer. He'd tried to give her the benefit of the doubt, but that was before he found out about her lies and the scheme that would have eventually parted him from a good chunk of the Laughlin fortune.

"How many people live on the Rusty Spur?" Tori asked, bringing him back to the present.

Eli started the truck and began to navigate the snow-packed road leading over the ridge to the valley floor below. "Counting me, you and Buck, there are ten of us that live on the ranch year-round. But during the summer months, I usually hire another five to ten men to help out with cutting and storing hay and mending fences, as well as working during fall roundup."

"I would have thought you'd need more than that from the size of this place," she said, her soft voice still filled with amazement.

"Contrary to popular belief we don't do everything on horseback or we would need more hired hands."

"Really?"

She sounded almost disappointed and confirmed his suspicion that she had little, if any, knowledge of how a modern ranch or farm operated. But he wasn't going to call attention to the fact. For one thing, they were already married—he had taken the plunge and planned to give it a shot. And for another, he wanted to see just how long it was going to take before she admitted that she knew nothing about rural life and what excuse she was going to give him for misrepresenting herself.

Her false claims might have been cause for concern, were it not for the iron-clad prenup they had signed before the wedding ceremony. That was his insurance. It not only protected his assets—the one-month get-acquainted period also gave him the time to figure out why she had answered his ad when she clearly wasn't qualified, as well as why he couldn't seem to bring himself to confront her about it.

"We use pickup trucks and four-wheel ATVs for a lot of the things that we used to have to do on horseback," he explained, noticing that she was paying extremely close attention to what he said. "But we do ride horses to move some of the herds to the summer pastures in the upper elevations. Most of those are areas that can't be reached on wheels."

"Herds?" She looked intrigued. "How many cows do you have?"

He laughed out loud. "I have four herds of *cattle*—two of registered Hereford and two of Black Angus. And since we raise our own working stock, I have a herd of quarter horses, as well."

"I meant *cattle*." Her cheeks colored a pretty pink and he knew she realized she had slipped up.

When he stopped the truck at the side of the house, Eli got out to open the passenger door. Placing his hands at her waist, he lifted her down from the truck. He had no idea why he kept picking her up, other than the fact that he liked the way she felt in his arms.

After he set her on her feet, she continued to hold on to his biceps as she stared up at him. It took monumental effort on his part to keep from drawing her to him for another kiss. "Why don't you go on inside out of the cold while I get your luggage?" he finally asked.

She stared at him a moment longer before nodding and turning to walk up the steps.

As he watched her cross the back porch to open the door, Eli exhaled, then took in a deep breath of sharp winter air. Why was he so damned turned on by Tori? She had clearly lied to him about her qualifications when she applied to be his wife. But the strangest part was that he didn't mind. Somehow it didn't seem nearly as important to him that the woman he chose be able to help around the ranch as it had been when he'd posted the ad online.

Reaching into the bed of the truck, he pulled out the two suitcases he had placed there when he'd picked her up at the airport, and started toward the house. There was something about Tori—a vulnerability, and quite possibly even a desperation—that had him overlooking her deception and making him want to shelter her from whatever she was running from. And he had no doubt there was something that compelled her to dive head-first into the uncertainty of being an email-order bride.

Why else would a beautiful woman, who was obviously born and bred to a more genteel life—a woman who could easily have just about any man she set her sights on—answer an online ad to marry a stranger and live on a remote ranch in the mountains of Wyoming?

He had a basic background check run on all of the applicants before starting the interview process and nothing had turned up in Tori's that had raised a red flag. But that didn't mean there wasn't something there and luckily he knew exactly whom to contact if he decided he needed to know more. Blake's older brother, Sean, had been an FBI agent for years before retiring to open his own private-investigation agency. One phone call was all it would take and within a week or so, he would know all about Tori.

Then, with whatever information Sean Hartwell was able to gather on her, he could decide if he wanted to try to make the marriage work or have it annulled and resume his search for a suitable wife.

As Tori walked toward the house, she chastised herself for her slipups. Since the FBI had confiscated her laptop, she'd had to make a special trip to the library to do extensive research on the Western way of life and the terminology used on a ranch. Calling a herd of cattle "cows" was the kind of mistake she couldn't afford to make again. Otherwise, Eli would realize she was a fraud and send her back to Charlotte faster than she could blink.

Glancing up at the Welcome to Our Home sign beside the back door, she sighed. It reminded her that she no longer had a home to go back to. Her father was dead, his business no longer existed and her so-called friends had abandoned her at the first sign of the scandal. If that hadn't been enough to convince her to change her name and relocate, the death threats from some of her father's former clients had. Even though she hadn't been involved in any of his illegal practices, her last name alone had been enough to incite hatred in people who didn't know her.

Then there was the matter of supporting herself. Her name was a huge strike against her, of course. But the fact that she had worked at her father's agency kept anyone in the banking-and-investments industry from considering her for a job, even though she had actually been instrumental in bringing down his house of cards.

With exactly four hundred and seventy-two dollars between herself and living in a cardboard box beneath a bridge, not to mention the chilling threats to her life, she'd had no other choice. She hadn't wanted to tell Eli so many fibs, but when she stumbled across his online ad while searching for an area of the country that might be safe, she had not only been intrigued, she had been desperate. Even her condo and car, which had been owned by the Bardwell Investments Agency, were about to be confiscated by the authorities to be sold in order to help with the reimbursement of her father's clients. Within a few weeks, she would have been homeless and with no means of transportation to go elsewhere.

Opening the door, she walked into a small mud-room and looked around. A built-in log bench had been constructed along one wall with cubbyholes beneath for boots and shoes. When she glanced at the opposite wall, she had to smile at the use of horseshoes turned sideways and attached to the wall to create hooks for coats and jackets. It was unlike anything she had seen in Charlotte and was perfect for a rustic Western ranch house.

Slipping off her coat, she hung it on one of the horseshoe hooks and opened the door leading into the kitchen. It amazed her how vastly different decorating preferences were in different areas of the country. Having been raised in a world of elegant antebellum mansions, elaborate cotillions and formal garden parties, she was fascinated by the rustic, down-to-earth preferences of residents of the western states. Nothing seemed to go to waste and, considering how frugal she'd had to become in the past few months, that appealed to her.

"You must be Eli's new bride."

Lost in thought, the sound of the man's voice caused her to jump. She looked over to find an older gentleman standing at the stove, stirring a huge pot of something that smelled absolutely wonderful. "Yes, I'm Tori, and you must be Buck."

"Guilty as charged," he said, nodding. "Eli gettin' your things?"

"Yes." She smiled. "Is there anything I can do to help you finish up dinner?"

"Around here we call it supper," Buck corrected. "But if you're of a mind to, you could set the table."

"I'd be happy to do that." When he pointed to the cabinet where the plates were kept, she asked, "How many places should I set? Three?"

Buck nodded. "Sally Ann feeds the hired hands down at the bunkhouse."

While Tori set the table, she admired the rustic beauty of the kitchen. The wagon-wheel chandelier hanging over the big round oak table and the plank floor worn smooth over the years made her feel as if she had been transported back to the Old West. As she continued to look around, she marveled at how the river-rock wall behind the stainless-steel stove and the gray-marble countertops complemented the oak cabinets and natural log walls. She wouldn't have thought the use of nature's elements would create such a warm and cozy atmosphere, but that was the only way she could think to describe the welcome feeling of the spacious room.

"I'll take these upstairs and put them with the rest of your things," Eli said when he brought her luggage in from the truck.

"I meant to ask if my other things had arrived," she said, smiling. "But the day has been such a blur of activity, I didn't even think of it."

He nodded. "I picked up the boxes at the freight company last week when I went down to Eagle Fork to talk to the attorney about our agreement and make arrangements for your arrival."

A couple of weeks ago, she had shipped most of her clothes and the few mementos the authorities allowed her to keep when her father's mansion and possessions were auctioned off. It was disheartening to think that her entire life could be reduced to a few shipping crates and a couple of suitcases. But that was the sad truth of the matter.

"Thank you, Eli," she said, admiring the ease with which he managed the heavy luggage holding the remainder of her clothes. Turning back to Buck, she asked, "Is there anything else I can do to help?"

The old man smiled as he nodded toward the table. "Just have a seat and I'll dish you up some of the best beef stew you've ever had. I'm bettin' you're pretty tired and hungry from all that travelin' you did to get here."

"It smells wonderful, but I'll wait for you and Eli to sit down with me," she said, smiling back.

Buck stared at her for several long seconds. "You're nothin' like I pictured you to be," he finally said, shaking his head.

She wasn't quite sure how to respond. "Is that a good thing or a bad thing?" she asked cautiously.

"It had better be good," Eli said, walking back into the room. There was a warning tone in his voice and the air suddenly seemed filled with tension as the two men glared at each other.

"Might as well sit down and eat before it gets cold," Buck finally said, turning to remove some biscuits from the oven.

The hostility between the two men was undeniable, and Tori had a feeling she might be a big part of their problem. Buck probably hadn't approved of Eli's method of obtaining a wife.

"Do you want me to give you a few moments?" she asked uncertainly. "I can go upstairs and start unpacking."

Eli shook his head. "That won't be necessary." He held a chair for her, then sat down at the head of the table. "Buck gets this way in the wintertime. He hates being cooped up in the house and figures that if he's miserable, everyone else should be, too."

"You don't have to talk about me like I'm not here," Buck snapped as he plunked down a plate of fluffy biscuits on the table, then brought the pot of stew over to start filling their plates. He scowled at Eli a moment before turning to smile at her. "We don't eat real fancy, but I can guarantee it's good and there's plenty of it."

"It smells wonderful, Buck." She returned his smile. "I'm sure it's delicious."

She wasn't certain why, but she liked Buck. He might be gruff and extremely blunt, but she could tell by the kindness in his eyes that he was a good person.

"How did things go around here today, Buck?" Eli asked as he passed Tori the plate of biscuits. "Anything I need to take care of?"

"Jack called earlier this afternoon and it looks like that pregnant mare you've been watchin' is gonna foal sometime tonight." Buck ladled stew onto her plate. "Most of the boys over at the bunkhouse are down with the flu and Jack didn't sound all that healthy when I talked to him."

Eli frowned. "Is he with the mare now?"

"Yup. He said he'd stay with her until you got back

and could take over," Buck said, ladling another heaping scoop of stew onto her plate.

Her eyes widened as she stared down at it. Although the stew looked and smelled delicious, she couldn't possibly eat all of it.

"Excuse me, Buck," she said, hoping he wouldn't be offended. When both men stopped talking to turn their attention her way, she shook her head. "I'm sorry, but I won't be able to eat all of this."

"Aren't you hungry?" Eli asked.

"I'm ravenous, but I never eat this much," she explained.

"Don't tell me you're one of those women who doesn't eat enough to keep a bird alive," Buck said, his disapproval evident in the lines creasing his forehead.

She pointed to her plate. "I have a very good appetite, but honestly there's enough here to feed a starving lumberjack."

Eli laughed. "Eat what you want and leave the rest."

"I can't do that," she said, shaking her head. "That would be wasteful." She didn't want to tell him, but in the four months since her father's downfall and subsequent death, she had learned to be extremely conservative with her resources. Until then, she hadn't given a second thought to how much food she wasted or how much it cost. Now, as far as she was concerned, throwing food in the garbage was the same as throwing money away.

Both men looked at her with amused expressions a moment before Eli reached for her plate, then handed his empty one to Buck. "I'll eat this," he said, grinning. "Just tell him how much you want."

Tori wasn't sure what Eli and Buck found so amusing. But it didn't matter. It seemed to have lessened some of the tension between them and she was happy to have a more relaxed atmosphere while they ate.

As she dined on the most delicious stew she'd ever eaten, she listened to Eli tell Buck how he intended to handle the daily chores while the majority of his hired men were down with the flu. "I'll take care of checking on the cattle out in the pastures. Do you think you'll be able to feed the horses?"

Buck looked thoroughly disgusted. "I might be gettin' older and have a touch of arthritis, but if I can't handle feedin' a bunch of hay burners you might as well bury me. Of course I can feed the damned horses."

"Good. Tori, I'm going to let you take care of mixing up the milk replacer and feeding the bucket babies," Eli said, turning to look at her.

Apprehension streaked up her spine. She didn't even know what a "bucket baby" was. Before she could respond, the phone rang and Eli left the table to answer it.

"You don't have the slightest notion what a 'bucket baby' is or what to do with one, do you, gal?" Buck asked, his voice little more than a whisper as he reached over to pat her hand.

She caught her lower lip between her teeth as she shook her head.

"Don't worry—I'll talk you through it," Buck said, giving her a conspiratorial wink.

"Am I going to be taking care of calves?" she guessed.

He nodded. "I'll show you how to mix the powdered

calf's milk and the best way to hold the bucket. The calves will do the rest."

Relieved that she wasn't going to have to admit that she was a complete fraud her first day on the ranch, she smiled. "I can't thank you enough, Buck. Please don't tell Eli that I didn't know what he was talking about. It's just that—"

"Your secret is safe with me," he interrupted, giving her hand a gentle squeeze.

"I'm going to have to cut supper short," Eli said, returning to the table. "Jack is sicker than a dog and that mare is getting close to dropping her foal." He walked over to open the door to the mudroom. "Tori, I'm going to need your help. Change into some work clothes and meet me down at the horse barn as soon as you can. Buck, you'll need to take care of the calves after you get finished feeding the horses."

Before she could ask which barn he was talking about, Eli put on his wide-brimmed black hat and walked into the mudroom to get his coat.

"Which barn does he want me to go to?" she asked, hoping Buck knew.

"Go upstairs and get changed, while I take care of puttin' the rest of this stew in the refrigerator," Buck said, getting up from the table. "I'll walk you down there, then I'll take care of the bucket babies and the horses."

Hurrying upstairs, Tori wasn't even sure which room to look in for her clothes, but opening doors along the long hallway at the top of the stairs, she finally found the room where Eli had put her things. Opening her designer luggage, she rummaged through her clothes until she found a pair of jeans. Quickly changing into them, she put on a T-shirt and a sweatshirt over it for warmth. She wasn't entirely certain she would need the layers of clothing beneath her coat, but it was below freezing outside and she would rather be safe than sorry.

Looking around at her clothes scattered across the bed and the unopened crates, she regretted not being able to unpack and put her things away. But there wasn't time for that now. Eli needed her to help him and she only hoped she didn't make any major mistakes.

After she put her hair into a ponytail to keep it out of the way and pulled her boots back on, she ran down the stairs to find Buck waiting for her by the kitchen door. "Do you have a pair of gloves?" he asked.

"Yes." When she pulled them from the pocket of her ski jacket, he shook his head.

"Those are too dressy and won't protect your hands." He handed her a pair of leather work gloves. "These are more suitable for chores." He reached up to pull a sock cap on her head to cover her ears. "I'd ask if you have any experience helping a mare give birth, but I already know the answer."

"No…no, I don't." She followed him out of the house into the frigid night air. "I should tell you—"

"Don't worry about it tonight," he said as they walked across the yard toward a row of buildings. "You can tell me all about yourself when we have more time."

When Buck led her through a small door built into one of the much larger ones at the front of the horse barn, she looked around. Stalls lined both sides of the center aisle. The dim light in one of the enclosures at the far end was probably where Eli and the mare were.

"Thanks, Buck," she said, turning to give him a quick hug.

He patted her shoulder. "Just do everything Eli tells you to do and you'll do just fine, gal."

When Tori reached the stall, she found Eli, kneeling beside a mare lying on her side in the straw. The poor animal appeared agitated and in pain.

"What do you want me to do?" she asked.

"Move slowly and keep your voice low and even," he said, removing his coat to lay it aside. He knelt by the mare's hindquarters and started wrapping the tail with a narrow roll of gauzy-looking fabric. "Sit down by her head and try to calm her while I take care of things at this end."

"It's all right, sweetheart," she said, sitting beside the mare to rub her broad forehead. She wasn't sure of what she was doing or if it was right, but she was determined to do all she could to help the poor animal.

"I don't think this will take too long," he said, sitting back on his heels. "She's had a couple of foals before this one, but I want to make sure everything goes okay."

"I can understand why. She's beautiful." Tori crooned as she continued to pet the horse. "This is a big moment in your life, isn't it, girl?"

"I see the front hooves emerging," he said quietly.

She noticed that he didn't move to help the mare. "You don't have to do anything for her?"

"No, she's doing fine on her own and it's best to let nature take its course," he said, sounding distracted. "We're just here in case she has a problem."

It was probably something she would have known if she had as much experience at farming as she'd claimed. But thankfully, Eli was focused on making sure the mare wasn't having problems during the birth and had answered automatically without paying much attention to her question.

Once the colt slid out onto the soft bed of straw and Eli cleared the membrane away from its tiny muzzle, he unwrapped the horse's tail, then motioned for her to leave the mare to walk out into the barn aisle. "We'll keep an eye on them from here," he said quietly as he picked up his jacket and followed her. Closing the stall's half door, he smiled. "You did a great job. Thanks."

"I didn't do all that much," she said, smiling back at him.

She was relieved that she had passed her first trial of dealing with livestock and hadn't embarrassed herself by showing how little she knew. But it was Eli's unexpected praise that caused a pleasant warmth to spread through her.

A bit flustered by the feeling, Tori turned to peer over the top of the stall door. As she watched, the mare got up, then turned around to nudge her copper-colored colt with her muzzle.

"What's she doing?" Tori asked, hoping the animal wasn't trying to hurt her baby.

"She's trying to get the foal to stand up," Eli said, from just behind her.

The heat from his body and the intimate sound of his voice close to her ear sent a tingling sensation straight to the pit of her belly. How could she possibly feel such awareness this fast? Even if they were married, she hadn't much more than just met him.

"Is the foal a boy or girl?" she asked in an attempt to regain her equilibrium.

"A little filly," Eli said, draping his arm over her shoulders as they watched the tiny animal try several times to get up before it was successful. "Would you like to name her?"

"Really? You'll let me do that?"

He nodded. "Do you have an idea of what you want to call her?"

"Can I think about it for a little while?" she asked, watching the filly wobble her way over to the mare to begin nursing. It was a sight she knew for certain she would never forget and helped take her mind off the churning feelings Eli had aroused within her.

"Take your time. There's no hurry," he said, giving her a smile that warmed her all the way to her toes.

As they continued to stare at each other, Tori wondered why a man like Eli would feel the need to advertise for a wife. With his rugged good looks and disarming presence, she'd have thought he would have women lined up across the state just waiting for a chance to get him to look their way. And what had compelled him to offer her the job of being his wife over the other applicants?

When they spoke on the phone the first time, she had asked him why he had advertised for a wife instead of taking a more traditional route. He had given her a vague answer about not being able to take the time to find someone, but Tori doubted that was the case. With a ranch foreman and so many hired men to do the ranch work, not having the time was more of an excuse than it was a reason.

Lost in thought, her breath caught and she abandoned all speculation when he turned her to face him. The intent in his dark brown eyes was undeniable.

"When you look at me that way, it makes me think you want me to kiss you again," he said, his voice sounding so sexy it sent another streak of excitement coursing through her. Wrapping his arms around her, he pulled her to his broad chest. "Would you like that, Tori?"

Her heart skipped several beats and if she could have found her voice she would have told him that she would like that very much. But since she seemed incapable of speech, she simply raised her arms to his shoulders and nodded.

Reaching up, he took off his hat and placed it on a stack of straw bales by the stall. Then, lowering his head, he captured her lips with his.

Tori felt the immediate stir of anticipation that she had experienced the first two times Eli had kissed her. But as he possessively moved his mouth over hers, she realized this kiss wasn't going to be a chaste caress like the others. This was a man teasing and exploring as he learned more about the woman he held.

When he coaxed her to open for him, she parted her lips and the first touch of his tongue to hers sent a wave of heat flowing through her entire body. She had been kissed before, but not like this. Eli Laughlin's kisses were world-class and light-years ahead of her limited experience.

As he stroked her with such tenderness it brought tears to her eyes, Tori clung to him to keep from being lost. But when he pulled her closer and she felt the evidence of his desire pressed to her soft stomach, a shiver coursed through her and she felt as if she might melt into a puddle at his big booted feet.

"I think we had better check on the mare, then get back to the house," he said, breaking the kiss. His gaze held hers as he slowly put his hat back on. "It's late, and we'll have to get an early start tomorrow morning in order to get everything done."

After he made sure that the mare and colt were doing fine, they walked back to the house, and by the time they entered the mudroom, Tori felt completely drained of energy. "I don't think I'll have any trouble falling asleep," she said as she removed her coat and boots.

"I'm sorry it's been such a long day for you," he said, hanging up their coats. "But you know how it is when you have livestock depending on you to take care of them."

"Of course," she fibbed as they walked into the kitchen and started down the hall. She didn't have a clue about taking care of animals and she suspected he knew that. But she had made a commitment and was determined to hold up her end of their bargain. "What time should I set my alarm for?"

He shook his head as they climbed the stairs. "Don't worry about it. I'll wake you when I get up."

When they stopped at the door to the bedroom where her things were, Eli smiled. "Sleep well, Tori."

"You, too, Eli."

Her pulse sped up when he lowered his head to give her a quick kiss. "I'll see you in the morning."

Nodding, she went into the bedroom, closed the door behind her then leaned back against it. How on earth could she possibly be so attracted to a man she barely knew?

She hadn't counted on that. At least not so quickly.

She had hoped that by the end of their trial period there might be an indication—possibly even a spark of attraction—to help her know how to proceed. But the chemistry between them was beyond anything she could have imagined and more than a little disconcerting.

It would be wonderful if the attraction led to the lasting relationship that she had always longed for. But what if it was like a flash fire—flaring strong and bright at first, then just as quickly burning out?

Pushing away from the door, Tori shook her head as she stripped off her clothes. She took a quick shower, put on her pajamas, tucked the clothes she had unpacked earlier when she'd looked for her jeans in the dresser drawers and climbed into bed. It was too early to tell much of anything at this point. She would just have to wait and see what the next few weeks held for her with her new husband. And in the meantime, she intended to concentrate on learning all she could about taking care of animals and the ranching way of life. With nowhere else to go and no way to get there, she had to.

Three

When Eli knocked on Tori's bedroom door for the second time, he waited for several seconds before turning the knob and letting himself into the room. He wasn't entirely sure what the protocol was for a husband who was barely acquainted with his wife, but he figured entering her room to wake her was probably acceptable.

The light from the hall cast a glow over the bed and illuminated her petite form snuggled under the comforter. Walking over to the side of the bed, he gazed down at the woman he had married. Her long, golden-brown hair looked like silken threads spread over the pillow and had him wondering what it would feel like spread over his bare chest after they made love. His body hardened and he mentally chastised himself as nine kinds of a fool.

She had clearly misrepresented herself and why he

hadn't immediately bought her a ticket back to Charlotte when he'd met her at the airport, let alone gone through with the marriage, was still a mystery to him. But from the moment he'd laid eyes on her, he couldn't seem to stay focused on his goal and the reason behind his advertising for a wife. He needed a son to inherit the Rusty Spur, to carry on the Laughlin legacy of running one of the biggest privately owned ranches in the state.

He didn't want to take the time, nor had he been inclined to look for a woman, go through the motions of a courtship, then learn the hard way that she found the land he loved to be too rugged and remote or, worse yet, that she was after a chunk of the Laughlin fortune. By advertising online, he had thought he would be cutting out all of the uncertainty by letting the women who applied know up front that the ranch was to hell and gone from what most people considered civilization. He had also made sure they knew there would be an iron-clad contract, limiting what they would get if the union ended in divorce.

What he hadn't counted on was a woman desperate enough to lie about her knowledge of ranching in order to marry a man, sight unseen. What was a woman as sweet and beautiful as Tori even doing cruising websites like the Hitching Post? Nor could he understand why he had decided to spend the next month trying to find out what drove her to such an extreme. Why couldn't he put things in perspective where she was concerned and just send her on her way?

But for reasons he didn't want to analyze too closely, whenever he got within twenty feet of her all he could think about was holding her and kissing her sweet lips until they both collapsed from a lack of oxygen. Even now, he would like nothing more than to lie down beside her and pull her to him.

Shaking his head at his own foolishness, Eli reached down to touch her shoulder. "Tori, it's time to get up," he said, hoping he didn't startle her.

She murmured something that sounded like his name a moment before she opened her eyes, then blinking, stared up at him. "What time is it?"

"It's almost five," he said, checking his watch. "Buck will have breakfast ready in about ten minutes. You need to get up and get dressed. We have a long day ahead of us."

When she sat up and stretched away the last traces of sleep, she smiled. "I'll be down in a few minutes."

Eli wasn't sure why, but his boots felt as if they had been nailed to the floor. If he had thought Tori was beautiful yesterday when she'd first got off the plane and then later at their wedding, it couldn't compare to the way she looked now. With her hair slightly mussed and her eyes heavy-lidded from sleep, she looked as if she had just made love. The thought sent his hormones into overdrive and he had to force himself to turn and walk toward the door before she noticed he was having trouble keeping his body under control.

"I'll see you downstairs," he muttered as he stepped out into the hall and closed the door behind him.

What the hell had gotten into him? he wondered as he descended the stairs. It wasn't as if he had never seen a woman wake up before. And most of them had been wearing a whole lot less than a pair of pink flannel pajamas with butterflies on them.

But Tori managed to make flannel look sexy. Real sexy. Hell, he had a feeling she could make anything she wore look that way.

Entering the kitchen, Eli walked over to the coffee-maker to get a cup of the black brew, then sat down at his place at the table. Lost in thought, it took a moment for him to realize that Buck had said something to him.

"What was that?" he asked, looking up.

"I asked if Tori is on her way downstairs," Buck answered, grinning from ear to ear.

"What's wrong with you?" Eli asked, frowning. "You look like a deranged jackass."

Buck threw back his head and laughed out loud. "She's already got you tied up in a knot, doesn't she?"

"No."

"I thought I taught you better than to tell a lie," Buck said, chuckling merrily as he turned back to the stove.

"You're treading on thin ice," Eli warned, grinding his back teeth. "You've already had your say on what you thought about me advertising for a wife, and as much as I hate to admit it, you were probably right. You don't have to rub it in."

Shaking his head, Buck brought a plate of bacon, scrambled eggs and hash browns over to set it down in front of Eli. "I don't admit this very often, but I was wrong. That little girl upstairs is gonna make you a fine wife, boy. She's got a hell of a lot of try in her and a good heart, just like your momma had. She'll be good for you if you aren't too pigheaded about keeping things all business."

Eli wasn't sure he had heard correctly. "You're telling me that the all-knowing, always right Buck Laughlin is admitting he made a mistake?"

"Yeah, but don't expect it to happen very often," Buck shot back.

"I didn't know the two of you were related," Tori said from the doorway.

Eli glared at his father. "I figured you would have introduced yourself when she arrived yesterday."

"When she came inside, she asked if I was Buck and I said I was," his father answered, shrugging. "My last name never came up."

Shaking his head in complete disgust at his father's screwed-up reasoning, Eli hooked his thumb in Buck's direction. "Tori, meet my dad, Buck Laughlin—the orneriest old buzzard this side of the Mississippi."

"I don't think he's ornery at all. You just have a lot of wisdom that you feel you should share, don't you, Buck?" The warm smile she gave his father had the old guy beaming above three days' growth of scruffy gray whiskers like a pimple-faced teenager on his first date.

"Me and this little gal are gonna get along just fine," Buck said, nodding his obvious approval. "She understands me."

Eli couldn't believe the change in his father. For a solid week before he placed the online ad, Buck had argued with him nonstop in an attempt to get him to change his mind. He had railed that it was the worst way in the world to meet a woman. He had even gone so far as to give Eli the silent treatment for almost a full day when nothing else worked. That day had been one of the best Eli could remember since taking over the ranch when Buck retired.

"How do you like your eggs, Tori-gal?" Buck asked happily.

"Scrambled is fine, thank you," she answered.

While Tori and his father chatted like two old friends, Eli shook his head and put a forkful of hash browns into his mouth. He might as well have been eating sawdust for all the appetite he had.

For five years, he had listened to Buck criticize every decision he made about the ranch, financial investments and anything else his father could think to find fault with. Then Tori arrived and, in a little over twelve hours, she had charmed Buck into an agreeable old fool.

"Tori, while you feed the bucket babies, I'll check on the mare and her foal to make sure they're still doing all right," Eli said as he pushed away from the table. Scraping his plate, he put it in the dishwasher and went to get his coat. "You'll find the calves in the barn where we take care of sick and injured animals. The milk replacer will be in the barn's feed room. As soon as you get them fed, meet me in the equipment barn."

Without waiting for her to respond, he jammed his hat on his head and walked out into the predawn darkness. It wasn't that he didn't want Buck and Tori to get along. If he and Tori were going to stay together, it would be important for his wife and father to care about each other as family. Hell, it might even make the disagreeable old cuss easier to live with. But on the other hand, if things didn't work out between himself and Tori, he didn't want Buck to get emotionally attached. His father might be as irritable and grouchy as a grizzly with a sore paw, but Eli didn't want to see him get hurt.

What confused Eli the most was Buck's rapid turn-around. Normally when Buck took a stand, hell would freeze over before he changed his mind, even when proven wrong. So what had caused his change of heart? And why?

More determined than ever to find out all he could about Tori, Eli made a mental note to call Sean Hartwell by the end of the day. Then all he had to do was sit back and wait for the extensive background report to come back, telling him all of her secrets and the real reason behind his wife's presence on the Rusty Spur.

"Buck, I can't thank you enough for showing me how to feed the bucket babies," Tori said as she hosed out the pails she had used to feed the calves, then sanitized the nipples on the sides. "Daisy and Buttercup are adorable and I'm thrilled that I get to take care of them."

Buck laughed. "You've already named 'em, have you?"

"Everything needs a name," she said, nodding.

"Well, you did a fine job, no matter what you call 'em," he said, handing her a couple of plastic bags for the washed buckets to keep them clean until the next use. He took the wrapped pails, placed them on a shelf in the feed room and closed the door. "We're lucky the calves were a little older when they lost their mommas. We can get 'em on grain starter in another week and that'll make feedin' time a whole lot easier."

Buck had been so helpful, teaching her how to mix the powdered milk replacer with warm water and showing her the trick to holding the bucket for an eager calf to nurse the nipple on the side without slopping milk everywhere. She felt that she owed him an explanation. "Buck, I know you're wondering why I told Eli—"

"Let me tell you something, Tori," he said, holding up his hand to stop her. "I'm a fairly good judge of character and I could tell right away that you're a good person. You have your reasons for wanting to be here and it's none of my business what they are. You're helpin' out and doin' your best to learn." He patted her shoulder as they walked toward the barn door. "Eli's the one you need to be talkin' to about all that." He started toward the house. "Now, you hightail it on over to the equipment barn and help Eli get ready to take care of the cattle out in the far pasture while I go feed the horses. Then I'm goin' back up to the house. This cold weather is makin' my arthritis act up. Besides, I have to figure out what I'm gonna feed the two of you for supper tonight."

"Thank you again, Buck," she said, hugging him. "I'll see you a bit later."

As she walked the short distance to the barn where the ranch trucks and tractors were kept, she couldn't help but wonder why her own father couldn't have been like Buck. In the short time she had been on the Rusty Spur, Buck had shown her more kindness and trust than her father had in her entire life.

Letting herself into the long metal barn, Tori was surprised at how many large pieces of farm equipment were stored inside. On one side, trucks in various sizes were parked side by side and tractors, wagons and a variety of farming equipment lined the other.

"How are the calves doing?" Eli asked.

"They're doing fine." She walked over to where he

was fiddling with the front wheel on a large, big-tired pickup truck. "I've named them Buttercup and Daisy."

Looking over his shoulder at her, he grinned. "Don't try to do that with all the cattle. You'll run out of names."

"What are you doing?" she asked, wondering if it was something she should know.

"I'm locking the front hubs to four-wheel drive," he explained, moving around to the other side of the truck. He pointed down the row of trucks. "The newer ones have automatic hub locks."

"Why aren't you using one of those?" she asked, noticing that the truck he was working on had seen better days.

"Since we got several inches of new snow last night, the ruts leading to the back pasture have filled in." He straightened to face her. "This truck sits higher and we won't have as much trouble cutting new path."

"Wouldn't it make more sense to use one of those and a wagon?" she asked, pointing to a tractor with huge tires.

He shook his head. "I didn't figure you knew how to drive one of those."

"I'm driving?" The thought of driving a piece of equipment that big with no experience was daunting and if she had a choice, the truck was the less intimidating of the two. But an even bigger concern was that he knew she was out of her element with farm equipment. She chose not to respond to his assumption and hoped he didn't comment further about it.

He nodded. "I'm going to throw flakes of hay out to the cattle while you drive."

That didn't sound too difficult. She was a good driver and surely she could manage navigating the truck across a wide-open space.

"Go ahead and get in the cab out of the cold," Eli said as he finished with the front wheels. "I'll drive over to the barn where we keep the smaller bales of hay and load up the bed, then you can take over."

When Tori reached up to open the truck's door, it looked as if she might need a ladder to climb into the cab. Fortunately, she spotted a chrome step mounted just below the door and, grabbing the seat and the armrest, she managed to pull herself up into the truck.

"This sits a lot higher than the truck you used to pick me up at the airport," she said when Eli climbed in behind the steering wheel.

"That's why I'm hanging on to it," he said, starting the powerful engine. "We only use it when the snow is deep and the job is too small to fire up one of the tractors."

As he put the truck in gear, a sinking feeling came over her. The truck was a standard shift and she didn't have the slightest clue how to drive a vehicle unless it had an automatic transmission. But maybe if she paid close attention to how Eli handled it, she could quickly learn what to do when he turned the driving over to her.

"Have you decided on a name for the foal?" he asked conversationally.

"Mmm, no," she answered as she tried to concentrate on the pattern he went through to change gears.

"Is something wrong?" he asked, frowning.

"No, I'm just...thinking about what I should name

the foal," she lied, grasping the first excuse she could think of.

Eli stopped the truck to get out and open the wide doors of the hay barn, then backed it into the opening to start loading hay. Tori mentally reviewed what she had observed. It hadn't looked difficult, she concluded. As long as she took her time and didn't try to rush, she should be able to bluff her way through it.

Lost in thought, she jumped when he opened the passenger side door. "Slide over behind the steering wheel."

"I thought you were going to drive out to the pasture, and then I would take over," she said, feeling a bit of panic start to set in as she moved over to the driver side.

He gave her a smile that caused her pulse to speed up as he climbed into the cab. "I'll get out to open and close the gates so you don't have to wade through the snow."

Taking a deep breath, she reached forward at the same time she put her foot on the clutch, then pulled the gear shift up as she had seen Eli do. So far so good, she thought as she gripped the steering wheel. Then everything seemed to happen at once. She lifted her foot from the clutch as she pressed down on the gas pedal, sending the truck lurching forward a moment before the powerful engine sputtered and died.

Seeing no way around it, she bit her lower lip a moment before she confessed. "I can't drive a vehicle with a manual transmission."

Eli's wide grin surprised her. "I was wondering when you were going to admit that."

"How did you know?"

"Your gaze was glued to every move I made from the

moment I started the truck at the equipment barn. That was a fairly good indication," he said, smiling. "Plus the fact that you had a worried frown when I told you to drive out to the pasture." He reached over to touch her cheek with his gloved index finger. "Honey, you probably don't realize it, but whatever runs through that little head of yours is written all over your pretty face."

"Why didn't you say something before now?" she asked, miffed that he had let her make a fool of herself. She wasn't going to think about the fact that he had just said she was pretty or that he had used an endearment. It was much easier to stay angry with him if she didn't think about that.

"I wanted to see how long it would take before you admitted you've never driven a stick shift." He shrugged. "It's no big deal. I'll teach you on the way out to the pasture."

After showing her the proper way to start the engine, he leaned over to instruct her on the use of the gear shift. "Now that you know the standard H pattern of the gears, you'll need to ease your foot off of the clutch at the same time you slowly press down on the gas," he said, leaning even closer.

When she did as he instructed, his warm breath feathering across her cheek sent a shiver of excitement coursing through her. Without thinking, Tori immediately took her foot off the clutch and pushed the gas pedal all the way to the floor. Lurching forward, the truck engine revved a moment before it died again.

"That's okay," Eli said, patiently. "Try again. But this time, ease off the clutch as you press on the gas pedal."

"You're making it hard to concentrate," she said,

surprised that she had vocalized the thought. The only other times he had been that close to her were the few times he had kissed her. The thought sent a wave of longing through her.

"Why am I making it hard to pay attention to what you're doing?" he asked, sounding as if he already knew the answer.

"You just are," she muttered as she restarted the truck.

Eli brushed a strand of hair from her cheek with his finger, causing her skin to tingle. "Could it be that you want me to kiss you again?"

"No."

"Really?" He didn't sound as if he believed her.

"Yes."

"Are you sure?" he persisted. "Because being this close makes *me* want to kiss you."

Her heart skipped a beat. "But you haven't finished teaching me how to drive this truck and you said we had a lot to do today."

"You're right." Without warning, he leaned in closer to give her a quick peck on the mouth. "That will have to do for now." Pointing to the steering column he added, "Try it again."

Tori tried to ignore the suggestion that they would be resuming the kiss later and concentrated on driving the truck. Her third try really did seem to be the charm as she started the truck. Although it was a bit bouncy when it started moving forward, she managed to drive it to the gate that led out to the pastures without killing the engine. With each gate separating the massive fields, she seemed to get better at taking off and only ground the gears a couple of times as she shifted.

By the time they reached the farthest pasture and Eli had her stop the truck close to a large herd of red, white-faced cattle, she felt a lot more confident. "This isn't nearly as hard as I thought it would be."

"Nope." He smiled. "And since the men are still suffering with the flu, you'll get even more practice tomorrow."

"What am I supposed to do, just drive along while you throw out hay?" she asked when he opened the passenger door to get out.

He nodded. "Go slow. You probably won't even have to shift into second gear unless you drive into a snowdrift."

As she waited for Eli to climb into the back of the truck and cut the wire holding the first bale of hay together, she couldn't help but feel quite proud of herself. She was experiencing so many new things and actually feeling useful for the first time since her father's downfall. She was taking care of two sweet little calves, had helped deliver a foal and was actually driving a standard-shift truck through a field to feed cattle. And she had only been on the ranch for one day. Amazing!

"Okay, we're ready to go," Eli called.

Shifting the truck into first gear, she eased it forward and watched Eli in the rearview mirror as he began scattering the hay. He had explained on the way out to the herd that the majority of his cattle were wintering on the land he leased from the BLM at a lower elevation and were being watched over by some men he had hired for the winter. And that's when it hit her.

Eli wasn't just a hardworking rancher. He was a very wealthy hardworking rancher. Why hadn't she realized it before now?

The Rusty Spur Ranch was huge, and Eli had more cattle than some people had hair on their head. It stood to reason he had to have a sizable bank account to go with it all.

When the attorney outlined the terms of their pre-nuptial agreement, she hadn't paid much attention to what he said after he explained the clause concerning the "get acquainted" phase of their marriage. But as she thought back on it, she vaguely remembered something being mentioned about her getting money in the event of a divorce and less money if the marriage was annulled. Could the lawyer have said she'd get a million dollars if they divorced? Now that she was thinking back on it, it was possible that's what he'd said. She should have listened more closely, but at the time she had been so overwhelmed by everything that she had a hard time thinking past the fact that she was actually in Wyoming and getting ready to marry a total stranger. And besides, she wasn't concerned with what assets Eli had because if the marriage didn't work out, she didn't want anything that didn't belong to her going into the marriage anyway.

She would, however, be forced to take the ten thousand dollars he had specified she would receive for her time and trouble if the marriage was annulled—not because she wanted to, but because she had to. If she didn't, she wouldn't have any way to make a new start elsewhere.

Frowning, she glanced in the rearview mirror at her

new husband. She had thought when she left Charlotte that she would never again have to worry about money influencing any of her relationships, let alone her marriage.

Eli didn't seem to be obsessed with his wealth or even acknowledge that he was anything but a hardworking rancher. But she didn't know him that well. Would he eventually prove to be as obsessed with money as her father had been? Or would he look at her as being beneath him the way her former friends had done when they'd discovered that she was penniless?

Lost in her disturbing thoughts, Tori failed to notice that she'd steered the truck away from the path they had created when they'd driven into the pasture. As it became more difficult for the truck to go through the snow in first gear, the engine made a growling sound, then died.

"That's okay," Eli called from the back. "Just start it up and slowly steer it back into the ruts we made coming into the pasture."

When she started the truck and put it into gear, Tori released the clutch a bit too fast and the truck bounced forward before it began to run smoothly. Glancing in the rearview mirror to apologize to Eli for the rough start, she couldn't find him.

Tori turned in the seat to look over her shoulder, but Eli was nowhere in sight. Where was he?

Slamming on the brakes, she turned off the engine and got out of the truck to find him. There were several cows munching on the scattered hay nearby, and although she was thoroughly intimidated by their size,

Tori hurried around to the back of the truck to see if she could find Eli.

Her heart stalled at the sight of him lying completely still in the snow. His black cowboy hat lay several feet away and she hoped and prayed he didn't have a concussion.

"Oh, dear heavens," she whispered as she rushed over to him to kneel in the snow at his side. "What have I done?" Brushing his dark brown hair from his forehead, she begged, "Eli, please don't be hurt. I'm so sorry. Please wake up!"

He opened his eyes at the same time his arms encircled her waist and he pulled her down on top of his chest. Startled, Tori let loose with a cry that she was pretty sure could be heard down in Eagle Fork and sent the cattle galloping in the opposite direction.

"What was that all about?" He laughed.

"I thought you were hurt," she said, a mixture of relief and anger coursing through her at the same time. She was relieved he was all right, but irritated that he had let her think he wasn't.

"No, I meant with the truck," he said, smiling as he held her close.

"I was looking in the rearview mirror," she said, settling on a half-truth.

She had been glancing in the mirror from time to time, just not when she had veered off the path. It probably wouldn't be a good idea to tell him that she had become distracted by the thought that he was rich or that she had come to the conclusion she wanted nothing to do with people who were wealthy.

His grin widened. "So you were checking me out, huh?"

"I…didn't say…that. I was…oh, never mind." Why did she sound so darned flustered?

"So you were watching the cattle?" he asked, raising one dark eyebrow.

"No."

"Then you were checking me out," he said confidently.

"I was looking to see that you were still back there," she said stubbornly.

He shook his head. "I prefer to think that you were watching me." Cupping the back of her head with his hand, he drew her closer. "If I'd been the one driving and you had been in the back of the truck, you can bet I would have been checking you out, Tori."

His words against her lips caused her stomach to flutter and a lazy heat to flow through her. When he fused their mouths and began to tease her lips with his tongue to open for him, Tori ceased thinking about his wealth and her prejudices and concentrated on the way Eli was making her feel. They might have only known each other a day and been married for a little less than that, but in Eli's arms, she felt as if she were where she belonged for the first time in her life.

As he stroked and explored, her body seemed to hum with sensations and, melting more fully against him, she gave herself up to the feelings. She loved the contrast between them—his large frame to her smaller one, his hard masculine contours to her softer feminine curves.

"You have the sweetest kisses," he said, breaking

the caress to nibble his way to the hollow at the base of her throat.

It felt as if her temperature increased by a good ten degrees, and Tori was more than a little surprised that they weren't melting the snow beneath them. "I like when you kiss me, Eli," she heard herself say. "You make me feel cher—"

She stopped herself before she could tell him that he made her feel cherished and as if she really mattered to him. But it was too soon. Even though it felt true to her, they didn't know each other well enough to be admitting something like that just yet. And she still had to determine if he was like all the other rich people she knew.

"I make you feel what, Tori?" he asked, his dark brown gaze holding her captive.

"You make me feel…cheerful and young at heart," she said, hoping her laughter sounded genuine.

He continued to stare at her for several long moments before a slow grin appeared on his handsome face. "If you say so." Lifting her off his chest, he plunked her down in the snow. "Being from Charlotte, I'll bet you've never made a snow angel."

"No, I haven't," she said, laughing. When he told her what to do, he stood up and smiled as she lay in the snow moving as if she were doing jumping jacks.

"Okay, that's good." He helped her to her feet, then picked her up to carry her to the back of the truck. "Climb into the bed and look down at your first snow angel."

When she did, she couldn't stop smiling. "It's so

pretty and really does look like an angel. I wish I had a camera to take a picture of it."

"Here, use this," he said, handing her his cell phone.

His indulgent smile warmed her as little else could. He was doing all this just because he knew this was her first time really getting to play in the snow and that it would make her happy, not because he had a burning desire to make snow angels.

After she took the picture and he helped her down from the back of the truck, he opened the passenger side door and helped her climb into the seat. "Don't we have more hay to throw out to the cattle?" she asked.

"Nope, I had thrown the last of the hay about the same time you took that wrong turn," he said, laughing.

When he walked around the truck to slide into the driver's seat, she frowned. "I wouldn't think you would get cell service here in the valley."

"I don't." He started the truck and headed back the way they had come. "I have the phone for the times I go outside of the valley. That way Buck has a way to get hold of me if he needs something."

As he drove back toward the ranch headquarters, she glanced over at Eli and couldn't help but feel a bit envious of him. She and her father had never enjoyed a relationship like Eli and Buck had. She could tell the Laughlins argued and sometimes frustrated each other beyond words, but beneath it all they shared a deep, abiding love. Otherwise, Eli wouldn't carry a cell phone he couldn't use the majority of the time just so his father would be able to reach him when he was away from the ranch.

Tori sighed wistfully as she stared out the window.

She wanted to be a part of something like that—needed that sense of belonging.

If things worked out with Eli and they decided to stay married, she would have that. Or at least a semblance of it.

Part of the reason she'd applied to be his wife when she'd seen his ad was the fact that he wanted children. At least if they had a child she would have someone who loved her unconditionally. But would her child's love be enough?

When no answers came, she leaned her head against the glass and closed her eyes. The one thing she had on her side was time. She and Eli still had a month to decide if being married to each other was what they both wanted. Hopefully by the end of that time, she would have the answer and know how to proceed with the rest of her life.

Four

Two days after his men came down with the flu, Eli found himself thinking about Tori on his way back from checking on them. When he stopped to see about his foreman, Jack, Sally Ann had asked if Eli needed her help with anything. That's when he realized how much help Tori had been over the past few days. She had not only helped him tackle the endless chores of running a ranch the size of the Rusty Spur, she had done everything he had asked of her without question or complaint—from feeding the bucket babies to the thankless and dirty task of mucking out stalls. He knew she had to be dead on her feet every night when he finally kissed her at her bedroom door, then continued on down the hall to the master suite for his nightly cold shower.

After the men recovered, he needed to show her how much he appreciated all that she had done. Maybe he could take a day and show her some of the ranch that couldn't be seen except on horseback. Of course, that was contingent on her ability to ride.

Eli smiled as he backed the truck into the equipment barn. He couldn't help but wonder how she was going to bluff her way through riding a horse. And there wasn't a doubt in his mind that was exactly what she would try to do.

What he couldn't figure out was why she didn't just tell him that her claim to rural experience was completely fictitious and be done with it. But what puzzled him more than her clinging to the falsehood was the fact that he wasn't all that upset by her deception. Maybe his complacency was due to their prenuptial agreement and the knowledge that he didn't stand to lose all that much if they had the union annulled, not to mention that he was having her investigated and in a few days would know for sure if she were hiding something. Or it could be that his curiosity was getting the better of him and he wanted to see just how far she would go with trying to bluff her way through things. He had to admit that her trying to drive a standard-shift truck had turned out to be pretty amusing. He could only imagine how creative she would be with riding a horse for the first time.

"It should be interesting," he said, laughing as he closed the big double doors and headed toward the barn where Tori was feeding the orphaned calves. Maybe it would be a good idea to take her out for a short ride first and see just how limited her riding experience was before he took her on a ride into some of the rougher areas of the ranch.

"So you're the reason Tori hasn't had any trouble with the bucket babies," Eli said, when Buck stepped out of the barn just ahead of him.

His dad shrugged. "All I had to do was show her how to mix up the milk replacer and clean the buckets that first time. After that, she's been doing it herself."

"What were you doing today, showing her how much grain starter to give them?" Eli guessed.

"Yup." Buck grinned. "You know you're not gonna be able to turn those calves in with the rest of the herd when they're old enough, don't you?"

Eli frowned. "Why not?"

"Tori will be heartbroken if you do. She's named 'em and she talks to 'em like they're her babies." A nostalgic smile curved Buck's mouth as he shook his head. "Your momma did the same thing with the first set of bucket calves I gave her to raise."

"So what did you do?" Eli didn't remember his mother being overly sentimental about any of the livestock, except maybe her horse.

"I kept those three heifers in the feedlot until you were born, then turned them in with the rest of the herd," Buck said, rocking back on his heels. "Once she had you to take care of, your momma didn't think so much about the cattle. I figure it will be the same with Tori."

"Is this your way of telling me you want a grandchild?" Eli asked, raising one eyebrow. Buck had never been known to beat around the bush. When he wanted something his hints usually carried all the subtlety of a sledgehammer.

"Well now, that wouldn't bother me one damned bit

to have a couple of little kids running around," Buck said, looking thoughtful. "I hadn't thought of it until you mentioned it, though."

Eli wasn't buying his father's feigned innocence for a minute. Buck knew that the primary reason Eli had advertised for a wife was to have an heir to inherit the Rusty Spur when it came time for him to retire.

"It's a little early to start thinking about having a baby together," he said, shaking his head. "I've only known Tori for four days and we've yet to decide whether we'll try to make things work or if we'll go our separate ways."

"Any idea how long that's gonna take?" Buck asked, pressing the issue.

"That's between me and Tori," Eli answered, through clenched teeth. He wasn't going to tell Buck that he had hired Sean Hartwell to investigate her. For one thing, Buck had his mind made up that she was the woman for Eli. And for another, the last thing he needed was for Buck to mention something to Tori about the investigation. "Besides, I told you about the month for us to get to know each other before we make our decision."

"I didn't want you to go about findin' a woman the way you did, but you couldn't do any better than that little gal," Buck said, starting to walk toward the house. "It wouldn't take me a month to decide to grab hold of her and hang on tight."

"How the hell do you figure that?" Eli asked, losing all patience. There were times when his father's logic aggravated him to no end. "You don't know her any better than I do. When I first told you about the ad, you couldn't say enough about how my decision had disaster written all over it. You even refused to come to the wedding. I'd love to hear what brilliant notion changed your mind about that."

"You know that if there's one thing I've always been good at, it's sizin' up a person within a few minutes of meetin' 'em," Buck said, turning back. "Tori's a good little gal. She's just been through some tough times and it hasn't been that long ago."

"How do you know?" Eli had always had a lot of respect for Buck's opinion of people. He'd never known his father to be wrong when it came to judging a person's character. But there was always a first time for everything. "Did she say something?" he demanded.

Buck shook his head. "No, and it's not my place to go questionin' her about it. So don't ask me to."

"I had no intention of asking you to do that," Eli said, trying his best not to lose his temper.

Buck glared at him. "Good, 'cause I won't."

"You were about to tell me your reasons for thinking she's a good person," Eli prompted. There were times when trying to get something out of Buck was like trying to pull hen's teeth.

"I don't *think* she's a good person—I *know* she is," Buck said flatly. "But you can see it in her eyes. She's been hurt by something or someone. It's my guess she's still tryin' to find her way and get her feet back under her. So you shoot her some slack and give her a chance, you hear? Or you'll have to answer to me."

As his father continued on toward the house, Eli wouldn't have been surprised if steam was escaping from his ears. Buck had a way of saying things that never failed to set Eli's teeth on edge. At times, his father seemed to conveniently forget that Eli was a grown man and capable of forming his own opinions, as well as making his own decisions.

But as Eli began to calm down, he thought about what Buck had said. The first day he'd met her, he had picked up on the fact that Tori seemed vulnerable and a little unsure, and he had figured she was running from something. Why else would a woman as beautiful as Tori enter into an unconventional marriage with a complete stranger?

But for the life of him, Eli couldn't figure out what it would be. Nothing had turned up in the background check he had run before deciding she was the woman he wanted to join him on the Rusty Spur. When he had interviewed her two character references, they had both verified that she had never been married before, had never been in trouble with the law and was a good, honest, upstanding citizen. Had they lied? Had Tori been in a relationship that ended badly and they were covering for her?

Just the thought of some man causing her any kind of emotional pain or, worse yet, being physically abusive with her made Eli want to find the bastard and treat him to some pain of his own. But that didn't make sense. There was no reason for her to withhold something like that. And it didn't explain the lengths she had gone to, claiming knowledge about the way a ranch was run, in order to get him to choose her.

But if it wasn't a man that sent her running from Charlotte, then what was it?

He sighed heavily. Normally patience was one of his strong suits, but he suddenly found himself wanting Sean to hurry up and call with the details of his in-depth investigation of her.

"Eli, is something wrong?"

Looking up, he watched Tori close the barn door and walk over to him. "No, I was just waiting on you to finish with the bucket babies." He put his arms around her and decided it was past time they spent an evening together doing something other than working. Maybe talking about something besides ranch work and what chore he wanted her to do next would give him some answers to his questions. "How would you like to catch a movie tonight?"

"That would be great, but do we really have time to drive all the way down to Eagle Fork, watch a movie and then drive back before we have to get up in the morning?" she asked, looking doubtful.

Laughing, he shook his head as he released her and they started toward the house. "No, but I was thinking that a movie on Pay Per View and a couple of bags of microwave popcorn would be the next best thing."

"That does sound nice," she said, smiling. "I haven't seen a good movie in so long, I don't even remember when or what I saw."

"Then it's a date," he said, draping his arm over her shoulders.

Glancing down at her, he liked that he had made her smile. Why hadn't he thought to do something nice for her before now?

He would have been more than happy to blame his oversight on having to take up the slack while his men recovered from the flu, but he couldn't. The sad fact was that he was so out of practice at dating, he hadn't even considered that getting to know each other might be better accomplished with a little courting.

Thinking back, he tried to remember the last time he had been on an actual date. Had it been a year or more like eighteen months?

Frowning, he shook his head. He couldn't count the night last summer when he and Blake stopped for a beer at the watering hole in Eagle Fork after the rodeo in Cheyenne. Hell, he hated to admit it, but all he could remember about the woman he had spent time with was her unnaturally red hair. He wasn't proud of it, but he hadn't even been able to recall her name when he'd left her place the next morning.

Of course, it wasn't as if he had a lot of opportunity to take a woman out. Working long days on the ranch and living an hour and a half—two hours if he drove the speed limit—from the nearest town wasn't exactly conducive to cultivating an active social life.

But he'd been okay with that. At least he had been until he'd marked his thirty-fourth birthday and came to the conclusion that if the Rusty Spur was going to be passed on to a sixth generation of Laughlins, he needed to get busy and find a woman. He'd found one, all right, and while he waited on Sean's report he was going to spend time with Tori on a more personal level and see how much he could learn about her on his own.

"What movie did you decide on?" Tori asked as they ate supper. While she helped Buck finish preparing their meal and set the table, Eli had gone into the family room to check the listings of available movies.

"I didn't figure you would care much for the latest action-adventure film," Eli said, smiling.

She shook her head. "No, I have to admit that I'm not a big fan of those or the ones that after you watch them you end up hiding under the covers all night, hoping that daylight hurries up."

"You don't like thrillers. That's good to know." He grinned. "But you don't have to worry. There's a romantic comedy that I figured you might like."

"Are you going to watch the movie with us, Buck?" she asked, turning to the older man.

He gave her an odd smile as he shook his head. "Nope. I'm pretty tired and as soon as I get the dishwasher started, I think I'm gonna mosey on down the hall and go to bed."

"Are you sure?" she asked, not wanting him to think they were trying to exclude him.

She watched Buck stare at Eli a moment, then nod. "I'm sure." He grinned. "And don't count on me bein' around on Saturday night, either. That's my night to head over to the bunkhouse for poker and beer with the boys. I won't be back till sometime Sunday mornin'."

"Is that what you usually do on Saturday night?" she asked Eli, wondering if she would be spending the evening alone.

"No, that's about the only Buck-free night I get," Eli said. "I'm not giving that up."

"One of these Saturday nights, I'm gonna stay home just to irritate you," Buck shot back. His tone was just as adamant as Eli's.

Tori sensed that something had happened between

father and son that had them both on edge. She only hoped that she wasn't the cause of their tension.

As the conversation turned to things that had happened around the ranch and projects Eli had planned for the spring, they both seemed to be a little more at ease. By the time they finished eating, she had an idea that she hoped would be met with a favorable reception.

"I know that I might not be here in the spring," she said cautiously. "But if I am, would you have any objections to my planting a few flowers and maybe a little vegetable garden?"

Both men fell silent as they turned to stare at her as if they couldn't quite believe what she had asked.

Suddenly feeling awkward and as if she had spoken out of turn, she added, "I probably shouldn't have asked. I mean…I might not…" She stopped babbling and, sighing heavily, shook her head as she stared down at her plate. "Never mind. It was just a thought."

When Eli's hand covered hers, she raised her gaze to meet his. "If that's what you want to do, it's fine with me."

"That's only if we…"

His gaze held hers when she let her voice trail off. "Right."

"I think that would be right nice," Buck said, leaving the table to rinse his plate and put it in the dishwasher. "I'll even help you take care of it."

"Thank you, Buck." She took her and Eli's plates to the sink. "But maybe we should talk more about it a bit later."

As she helped load the dishwasher, Tori wondered if Eli thought she might have been a bit presumptuous. After all, they might have shared a few kisses that could have easily ignited the hay in one of his barns, but it was still too early to predict the outcome of their arrangement.

"The movie will be starting in a few minutes," Eli said, taking her by the hand.

"Buck is tired and I really should help him clean up the kitchen," she said, glancing at the few things left to put into the dishwasher. At first, she had wondered why with their wealth, Buck had taken over the housekeeping chores when he'd retired, instead of hiring someone. But one evening while she was helping him clean up the kitchen, he had admitted that he liked, as he put it, "putterin' around the kitchen" instead of sitting around with nothing to do.

"You go on ahead and watch your show." Buck waved his hand at the counter. "All I have left to do is wipe things off and start the dishes to washin'."

"Are you sure?" She didn't want to leave the impression that she wasn't willing to do her part in helping out.

"I'm positive." Buck patted her shoulder. "You've been workin' hard ever since you got here. Now, go enjoy your movie with Eli."

As he led the way into the family room just off the kitchen, she wondered if Eli would want to discuss her premature suggestion that she would like to plant a garden. But the more she thought about it, the more she realized that she had every right to assume she would still be living on the Rusty Spur in the spring. She had married Eli in good faith and with every intention of trying to make the union work. By making plans for the future, she was actually reaffirming her commitment.

"What are we going to watch?" she asked, feeling more confident. If he couldn't understand that she was willing to give their marriage every chance, well, that was his problem, not hers.

"I forget the title, but it has Julia Roberts in it," Eli said, leading her over to the big leather couch.

"I haven't kept up with movies, but I'm sure it will be good," she said, starting to sit in the matching chair flanking the couch.

"Where do you think you're going?" he asked, catching her hand in his.

"I wasn't sure…." Looking up at him, she sighed as she shook her head. "Eli, I…I'm not very good at all of this."

His frown indicated that he didn't have any idea what she was talking about. "What do you mean by that?"

"Everything about our situation is so unorthodox that I'm not sure what to do or what to say about anything," she explained, trying to gather her thoughts. "I'm your wife, but I don't know you that well. I might be married to you now, but I'm not sure if we'll be married by the time the snow melts." She shook her head. "I don't know whether to make plans or just live in a state of uncertainty until… To tell you the truth, I don't know when I'll start feeling more secure about this." Stopping, it was her turn to frown. "I don't even know where to sit."

He stared at her a moment with his piercing brown eyes, then, giving her an understanding smile, pulled her into his arms. "I'm just as unsure of the outcome as you are, honey. But I can tell you this much—I don't want you feeling like you have to walk on eggshells all of the time. Don't hold back. Tell me what you're thinking about our situation and how you feel about it, instead of holding it in and being unsure. It's the only way we'll be able to decide what to do when the time comes."

Feeling as if a weight had been lifted off her shoulders, she nodded. "That goes both ways. This effects both of us, and I need to know just as much about what you think and feel as you do about me."

He pulled her more firmly against him and lowered his mouth to hers. "You've got yourself a deal, honey."

As his lips settled over hers, Tori stopped thinking and started feeling. She had heard some of her former friends describe their boyfriends' kisses as intoxicating and, for the first time, she began to understand what that meant. Eli's lips moving over hers was like a drug and one that she could easily become addicted to.

Deepening the caress, he teased her into doing a little exploring of her own and when she tentatively stroked his tongue with hers, the groan that rumbled up from his chest filled her with a feminine power she hadn't known she possessed. Just the thought that she could bring Eli the same kind of pleasure that he did her when they kissed caused a tiny thrill to course through her.

Caught up in the heady feeling, it took a moment for her to realize he had picked her up. Then he lowered himself to the couch and set her on his lap. But the feel of his large hand slowly sliding from her waist to her knee, then back up the length of her to cup her breast caused an awareness that rocked her with its intensity. As he teased her tightening nipple through her clothing, she became aware of his hard arousal pressed to the side of her leg. It seemed they might not know much about each other, but their bodies didn't seem to have any problem communicating what they were feeling and what they needed from each other.

"I think we had better turn on the television and start watching the movie," Eli whispered against her skin as he kissed his way to her ear. "Otherwise, it's going to be a real marriage quicker than either of us anticipated."

The thought sent a shiver of longing through her like nothing she had ever experienced before. "Y-yes, that would be best," she stammered, moving off his lap.

Tucking her to his side, he draped his arm over her shoulders and used the remote to turn on the movie. As the show played, Tori found her gaze slipping from the elaborate home-theater system to the man seated beside her. He wasn't anything like the wealthy men she had known in Charlotte. For one thing, none of them worked even a fraction as hard as Eli. Over the past several days, she had watched him do hard manual labor from before sunup until sundown, without a hint of a complaint. And for another, none of the men she had been acquainted with, including her father, would have been content to stay at home to watch a movie. If they couldn't go to see the first showing in a theater, they simply wouldn't see the film at all.

Lost in thought, it surprised her when the movie ended and the credits began rolling up the screen. "That was good," she said, not knowing if it was or not.

Eli nodded. "It had its moments."

Feigning a yawn, Tori rose to her feet. "I suppose it's time I got to bed. The girls will be waiting on me tomorrow morning."

"Have you given any more thought to what you'd like to name the foal?" he asked, turning off the big-screen television.

She hadn't really had time to think of anything but what chores needed doing and how tired she was when she went to bed at night. "No, but considering her coloring, I think the name Copper would be appropriate."

He seemed to consider her suggestion as they walked toward the stairs. "That sounds like a pretty good name for a sorrel filly."

Unfamiliar with the term, she made a mental note to look it up on the internet the first chance she got. She assumed he was talking about the foal's reddish-orange color, but she needed to be sure.

When they stopped at her bedroom door, he used his index finger to brush a strand of hair that had escaped her ponytail from her cheek. "Tomorrow afternoon, I'll saddle a couple of horses and we'll ride out to the pasture to chop the ice at the edge of the pond."

For the past few days, whenever they went to take hay to the cattle, they had stopped at the edge of a huge pond to chop holes in the ice for the cattle to get a drink. "Won't the cattle need hay?"

She hoped that riding a horse wasn't difficult. She had ridden once, as a child. But that had been in an indoor arena at a friend's birthday party and an adult had led the horse around with a rope tied to its halter.

"Most of the men have recovered from the flu and will be taking over their chores again tomorrow," he said, his brown eyes darkening as he lowered his head to give her a kiss that sent her temperature soaring.

When he finally raised his head, he smiled. "Sleep well, Tori."

As she watched him walk down the hall to his room, she barely resisted the urge to fan herself. If his kisses were any indication, his lovemaking would surely cause her to burst into flames.

A shiver coursed through her and she wasn't entirely sure if it was from the desire he created within her or the fear of what he would discover about her in the weeks ahead. Either way, she had a feeling it wasn't going to take long for a definitive answer about whether they were going to try to stay together. She only hoped that he understood when she explained about her father and her reasons for running from the only life she had ever known.

From the corner of his eye, Eli watched Tori size up the little mare he had saddled for her to ride. Smaller than most of the working stock and with a gentle temperament his men referred to as "lady broke," she would be easy for a novice to handle. And he had no doubt Tori had never ridden before. One look at the panic on her beautiful face last night when he'd mentioned going for a ride had convinced him of that.

"Go ahead and mount up," he said, pulling the cinch tight around his gelding. "It won't take but a minute and I'll have my horse saddled."

"I can't," she answered.

He stepped around the gelding to see what the problem was. "Why not?"

"The horse is too tall. I can't get my foot high enough to put it in the stirrup," she said, shrugging. She didn't look all that upset. In fact, she looked downright relieved.

"How did you mount your horse back in North Carolina?" he asked, barely able to keep from grinning.

Eli didn't have any idea why he found her trying to bluff her way through everything so darned cute when she was clearly trying to deceive him. But he did and he couldn't wait to see how she handled this situation.

"Someone always helped me," she answered.

Walking over to where she stood at the mare's side, he placed his hands at her waist and lifted her, finding himself staring at the designer label on her cute little blue-jeans-clad backside. Calvin Klein had never looked so good, or so tempting.

"Throw your leg over the mare's back," he said, wondering how much longer he was going to be able to tolerate his nightly cold showers. Even those didn't seem to be as effective as they had been when he'd first brought her home.

When she sat in the saddle, her smile looked strained. "I'm ready when you are."

Oh, he was ready all right, but not for horseback riding. Forcing himself to move, Eli walked back over to the gelding and finished securing the cinch, then swung up into the saddle.

"Lead the way," he said, shifting in the saddle to relieve the pressure of his arousal in his suddenly too-tight jeans. If he didn't get his mind off his wife and her enticing body, he was going to end up doing permanent damage to himself.

"I'd rather you lead the way," she said, sitting ram-rod straight in the saddle.

Reining the gelding over beside the mare, he asked, "Honey, when are you going to admit that you've never been on a horse before?"

"But I have," she insisted. "Just not recently."

"How long are we talking here?" he asked doubtfully.

"A few years." She sighed. "But I'm sure it will come back to me."

Laughing, he shook his head as he urged the gelding into a slow walk. Once he got her to admit that she didn't know the first thing about riding a horse, he'd teach her to ride. But he had to give her credit for one thing. Tori might be short on experience, but she sure didn't suffer the lack of courage to try.

The mare followed the gelding just as he knew she would and in no time they were making their way out of the ranch yard toward the first pasture gate. Slowing his horse, he rode alongside Tori.

"Is it coming back to you?" he asked.

"It's just like riding a bicycle," she said, nodding.

"Yup. Once you learn you never forget." He didn't want to add to Tori's apprehension by reminding her that the "bicycle" she was riding now had a mind of its own, and although she was the most gentle horse on his ranch, the mare—like any animal—still had the potential to be unpredictable.

By the time they reached the pond, he could tell that Tori had relaxed a little and even loosened the death grip she'd had on the saddle horn from the moment he'd lifted her into the saddle.

"You don't have to dismount," he said, swinging down from his horse to untie the ax he had secured to the back of the saddle. "I just thought you might like to go for a little ride and enjoy yourself for a change instead of having to work all day."

"Thank you." She smiled. "We've been so busy since I arrived, I can hardly believe it's almost been a week already."

He nodded as he swung the ax down to break the ice at the edge of the pond. "Now that most of the men are back to work, it should slow down quite a bit."

"Eli? I...uh, I think...I need your help."

He looked up, hearing the panic in Tori's voice. When he spotted her and the mare, his heart felt as if it came up in his throat. Tori had apparently let the mare have her head while she waited on him to finish with the ice. With no guidance, the mare had wandered onto the ice and they were a good ten feet out onto the pond's frozen surface.

Five

"Whoa, Ginger," he said in a calm, yet firm voice. He didn't want to startle Tori or the mare, but he had to get them back on solid ground. Although fairly thick, the ice could still have thin areas and soft spots where the sun's rays had weakened it.

When the mare came to a halt, he hoped his voice sounded calmer than his insides felt. "Tori, the mare is trained to neck-rein. I want you to lay the right rein on her neck. She'll turn around. Then I want you to slowly walk her back to the bank."

Had he been on the mare, he would have pulled back on the reins and, using pressure from his knees, backed her off the ice to solid ground. But teaching someone to get a horse to back up wasn't something he wanted to try doing on the surface of a frozen pond. Nor did he dare walk out on the ice to lead the mare back. Adding his weight could tip the balance and cause the frozen surface to give way.

"We're going to…make it, G-Ginger," Tori said to the mare. She didn't sound at all certain.

"That's right, honey," Eli said, doing his best to sound reassuring. "Just a few more feet."

Tori and the mare were almost to the bank when he heard the sound that sent fear like Eli had never known surging through him. The ice was beginning to give under the mare's weight and the sickening crack seemed louder to him and more ominous than a clap of thunder.

"Tori, honey, stay focused on me and you'll be off the ice in no time," he said, careful to keep his voice even.

The words had no sooner left his mouth than the ice gave way beneath the mare's back legs, and he watched in horror as Tori slid off the back of the horse into the icy water. Fortunately, they had made it close enough to the bank that the water wasn't more than a few feet deep and she only sank up to her abdomen, but with the outside temperature below freezing, hypothermia setting in was a danger that he didn't even want to contemplate.

Pulling Tori out of the water, he immediately put his hat on her head and tied the bandanna in his coat pocket at the back of her head to keep her nose and mouth covered. He knew she probably wondered what he was doing, but he needed to keep as much of her body heat from escaping as he possibly could.

"Wh-what…are…y-you…d-doing?" she asked, her teeth chattering so badly he could barely understand her when he started stripping her of her wet clothes.

"It's going to be all right, honey," he tried to reas-

sure her. He had to keep her as warm as possible until
he could get her back to the house.

His heart hammered at his rib cage as he threw her
wet coat aside, then peeled her sweatshirt and T-shirt
from her violently shivering body. Taking his shearling
coat off, he wrapped her in it, then turned his attention
to catching the frightened mare. Quickly unsaddling
the animal, he grabbed the saddle blanket, still warm
from being between the saddle and the mare's broad
back, and wrapped it around Tori's legs.

Lifting her onto the back of the gelding, he swung
up into the saddle behind her, then settled her on his
thighs and cradled her to him. "Hold on, honey," he said
as he kicked the gelding into a run. "We'll be back at
the house in a few minutes."

They weren't more than a quarter of a mile from the
house, but the distance had never felt as far or the horse
as slow as at that moment. In a matter of minutes they
were across the pasture and entering the ranch yard.
It felt like hours.

Eli rode the gelding up to the back porch. Dismount-
ing, he carried Tori into the house. "Call Jack to send
one of the men out to the pond to get the mare and another one to take care of my gelding," he ordered as he
passed Buck. "Then throw some blankets in the clothes
dryer to heat them."

"What happened?" Buck demanded, following him
down the hall to the stairs.

"Tori fell through the ice," he said, taking the stairs
two at a time.

He bypassed her room and carried her straight to
the master bedroom. Setting her on her feet, he dis-

carded his hat, the bandanna and the saddle blanket, then pulled off her boots and socks and stripped off the rest of her clothing.

"N-no...s-stop," she stammered, trying to push his hands away.

"It's okay, Tori. I have to get the rest of these wet clothes off you," he said, sounding far calmer than he felt. He was encouraged that she tried to protest. At least she hadn't slipped into a state of confusion, which would indicate more than just a mild case of hypothermia.

"S-so...c-cold," she said, shaking all over.

"I know, honey," he said, getting one of his long-sleeved thermal undershirts from the dresser to pull over her head.

He knew his long underwear would be way too big, but it was the best he could do. He helped her pull the thermal pants on, put a knitted wool beanie on her head and thick socks on her feet, then picked her up to carry her over to the bed.

"You'll start to get warm in just a few minutes." Once he had her covered with the comforter, he kissed her cool cheek. "I'll be right back," he said, going straight to the medicine chest in his bathroom.

Returning with the digital thermometer, Eli placed it to her ear and waited until he heard it beep. He breathed a sigh of relief when the reading was only a couple of degrees below normal—meaning her core temperature was a degree or two warmer. Taking her pulse, he was glad to find it to be strong and regular.

"Is she gonna be all right?" Buck asked, when he

entered the room with his arms full of thick blankets. His expression was as concerned as Eli had ever seen.

"I think so. It's a mild case of hypothermia," he said, pulling the comforter back to spread the heated blankets over Tori. Covering her and the blankets with the comforter, he shrugged out of his shirt. "I got her out almost as soon as she hit the water, and she only went in up to the middle of her abdomen."

"How did it happen?" his father demanded, his scowl indicating that Eli should have been watching her more closely.

"It's a long story," Eli said, reaching to unbuckle his belt. "We'll talk later. For now, make her some of that herbal tea with honey you seem to think is a cure-all. If nothing else it will help warm her from the inside out and give you something to do besides question me."

Without waiting for Buck to respond, Eli sat on the side of the bed to remove his boots and socks, then shucked his jeans and underwear. Climbing into bed beside her, he pulled Tori into his arms.

"Wh-what are...y-you doing?" she asked, even as she turned on her side and snuggled deeper into his arms.

"I'm sharing my body heat with you."

"Y-you took off...m-my clothes." Her tone might have sounded more accusatory if her teeth weren't still chattering like a set of castanets.

"And I'd do it again if I needed to," he said, nodding. He checked to make sure the warmed blankets were tucked in around her neck. "Raise your leg, honey."

"Wh-why?"

"I'm going to put my leg between yours to help warm

the blood flowing through your femoral arteries," he answered.

When she did as he directed, Eli slipped his thigh between hers and immediately wondered what kind of miserable bastard he had become. Her soft body felt absolutely wonderful and his began to stir in response as she moved even closer to him.

How could he possibly get turned on in a situation like the one they were in at the moment? Tori needed the warmth of his body, not his unwarranted lust. Using every ounce of strength he had in him, Eli fought to control his runaway hormones as he held the shivering woman in his arms.

"Thank you…Eli," she said, a few minutes later. "You saved…my life."

Her words caused him to feel as guilty as hell. If he had called her on the bluff about knowing how to ride, instead of letting her continue the ruse, the accident wouldn't have happened. What if the ice had given way when she was farther from the pond bank? What if he hadn't been able to get her out of the water and back to the house as quickly as he had?

Eli squeezed his eyes shut against all of the what-ifs and took a deep breath. If she had been harmed in any way by his negligence, he would never forgive himself.

"You're safe now, Tori," he finally managed to say around the fist-sized lump clogging his throat.

"How did you know what to do?" He was relieved to hear her teeth had stopped chattering and her shivering had eased up a bit.

"Living in this climate and this far from town, medical assistance isn't immediately available," he said, kissing her forehead. "Out here, we have to learn early on to be cautious and know what needs to be done in an emergency situation because it could mean the difference between life and death."

She nodded. "I'm glad you knew what to do."

He started to tell her that if he hadn't been so cavalier about her riding abilities the accident wouldn't have happened to begin with, but a knock on the door stopped him. "Come on in, Buck."

"How's she doin'?" his father asked, walking over to set a steaming mug of herbal tea on the bedside table.

"Thanks to Eli's quick thinking, I'm going to be fine, Buck," Tori said, her voice sounding a lot stronger. "I'm not nearly as cold now."

"I'm glad to hear you're gonna be all right," Buck said, nodding.

"Could you hand me the thermometer?" Eli asked his father. He wanted to check her temperature again to make sure it was still rising.

"When you make sure Tori's settled, I'd like to talk to you downstairs," Buck said, handing Eli the thermometer. Without waiting for his response, Buck walked out of the room.

As he took Tori's temperature, Eli had a good idea what was on Buck's mind and knew he was in for a good tongue-lashing for letting something happen that put Tori in jeopardy. It was no more than he deserved and for once, he wasn't going to resent Buck's criticism. Tori wasn't familiar with the harsh climate and had no idea the danger she had been in. But he did and his carelessness could have cost her her life.

An hour later, after she'd drunk the herbal tea and

stopped shivering, he took her temperature and thanked the heavens above that it was back up to normal. "How are you feeling now, honey?" he asked as he took her pulse. It was regular and strong.

She pulled the wool cap from her head. "I'm getting hot and I feel like I need a nap."

"That's good," he said as he sat up on the side of the bed and reached for his clothes. "Your temperature is normal and you're tired because your body used a lot of energy in an attempt to stay warm."

"You wouldn't allow me to go to sleep earlier," she said, yawning. "Is it safe for me to take a nap now?"

He nodded as he stood up to zip his jeans. "Go ahead and get some rest. I'm going downstairs to talk to Buck for a few minutes, but I promise I'll be here when you wake up."

He tucked his shirt into the waistband of his jeans and leaned over to kiss her. Her eyes were tightly closed and her cheeks were a rosy-pink. "Is something wrong?"

"No."

"Then why do you have your eyes scrunched shut and why is your face red?" He had a feeling he knew.

Her cheeks turned an even deeper shade of pink. "I didn't realize I was lying in the arms of a naked man."

"You can open your eyes now, Tori. I'm fully dressed." When she did, he grinned. "Just so you know what to expect, the next time you're lying in my arms in this bed, I won't be the only one with my clothes off."

Her eyes widened and he had the distinct impression that he had just rendered her speechless.

Giving her another quick kiss, Eli forced himself

to move before he took off his clothes again and got back in bed. She needed her rest and he needed to get Buck's lecture out of the way so he could be there when she woke up.

The next morning, Tori woke to daylight for the first time since arriving on the Rusty Spur. Glancing at the clock on the bedside table, she threw back the covers and got out of bed. It was a little past eight and she should have fed the calves a couple of hours ago.

As she showered and got dressed, she thought about the day before and her brush with disaster. It was her own fault. If she hadn't tried to fake her way through riding the mare, she wouldn't have been in the position to fall through the ice in the first place. Thank heavens Eli had known what to do. Otherwise, she could have very easily been in serious trouble. But there hadn't been any hesitation on his part and because of that, she had suffered nothing more than mild hypothermia and no small amount of embarrassment.

Her cheeks heated. She still had a hard time believing that he had seen her as naked as the day she was born. Of course, when he got out of bed after sharing his body heat to help her get warm, she had been treated to a view of his bare muscular backside.

A tingling flutter in the pit of her stomach reminded her of just how magnificent it was, too. His broad back and shoulders were perfectly defined with muscles made hard from years of ranch work. And his rounded bottom and long muscular legs could have belonged to Michelangelo's statue of David.

She shook her head as she hurried downstairs. If she

had that kind of reaction from a glimpse of his back-side, what would happen if…?

"Don't go there," she said aloud.

Entering the kitchen, Tori found Buck sitting at the kitchen table drinking a cup of coffee as he looked through a seed catalog. "Mornin', Tori-gal," he said, looking up. "What would you like for breakfast?"

"Good morning, Buck." She shook her head. "I won't have time to eat. I should have been up hours ago to feed the calves."

"They've already been took care of," he said, rising from the chair to walk over to the stove.

"Oh, Buck, I'm so sorry you had to—"

"Don't thank me," he said as he reached for a skillet hanging from the pot rack above the butcher-block island. "Eli said he'd take care of 'em and that I was to let you sleep until you woke up."

"I should probably go see if he needs help with something," she said, starting to get her coat. But when she started into the mudroom, she remembered that Eli hadn't taken the time to retrieve it when he'd brought her back to the house to warm up. "I don't have a coat anymore."

Bent over to get a carton of eggs from the refrigerator, Buck smiled over his shoulder at her. "One of the boys brought it and your clothes back to the house when they went to get the mare. I already got 'em washed and they're dryin' now." Straightening, he asked, "How 'bout I fix you some scrambled eggs, a steak and some biscuits and gravy?"

"It sounds wonderful, but I hate for you to go to all that trouble." She got a coffee mug from the cabinet above the coffeemaker and poured herself a cup. "I'll just have coffee and toast."

"Can't gain your strength back eatin' like a bird," Buck said, his tone disapproving. "Just tell me one thing. If I fix it, will you eat it?" The eggs were already sizzling in the pan.

"Yes, but—"

He pointed to the table. "Sit."

Realizing it was futile to argue with him, Tori sat in her chair at the table. "As soon as my coat is dry, I'll try to find Eli and find out what he wants me to do today."

"He said you weren't to leave the house," Buck answered, opening the oven door to pull a tray of biscuits out that he'd tossed in to warm up. He turned to face her. "Normally, I'd call him on bein' high-handed, but in this case, he's right. You don't have any business bein' out in the cold just yet."

"I'm fine," she said, frowning.

He nodded as he brought her plate over to set it in front of her. "And we want to make sure you stay that way."

Sighing, she wondered what she would do for the rest of the day as she ate the delicious breakfast Buck had made for her. Since her arrival, she'd spent almost every waking minute taking care of animals or helping Eli with one chore or another. It was amazing how quickly she had become accustomed to the physical activity.

When she finished her meal, she reached for the catalog Buck had been looking at earlier. "Do you mind if I look at the seed catalog?" she asked.

"Go right ahead." Buck smiled as he brought his cup of coffee over and sat down at the table with her. "I got it in the mail a while back and decided to start lookin' to see what we might plant in the garden come spring."

She hated to remind him that she might not be around then, but she supposed it wouldn't hurt to start making plans just in case she was still living on the Rusty Spur. And even if she wasn't, Buck might want to go ahead with the project.

As she and Buck discussed the size of the garden and how much they should plant of each type of vegetable, Eli came in from outside. Hanging up his coat, he walked over to get a cup of coffee before joining them at the table. "Did you sleep well?"

"I slept fine, but you should have woken me to feed the girls." She smiled as she thought of the two red-and-white bucket babies. "How were Daisy and Buttercup this morning? Did you scratch Daisy's back? She loves that. And Buttercup likes for me to rub her forehead." When she noticed the two men exchanging a look, she paused for a moment. Buck wore a smug expression, while Eli was glaring at his father. "Is there something wrong with me bonding with the animals I'm taking care of?"

"Not at all, honey," Eli said, reaching over to take her hand in his. "I think it's nice that you care about them."

"Me, too," Buck added, his eyes looking suspiciously misty.

Checking his watch, Eli got up to refill his coffee cup. "As much as I hate to do it, I have to work on the ranch books today."

"Is there anything I can do to help?" she asked. Doing boring paperwork would be better than having nothing to do at all for the rest of the day.

"You can keep me company if you'd like." Eli's smile made her feel as if the temperature in the room went up several degrees.

"Buck, if you'll let me know when it's time, I'll help you make lunch," she said, rising from the chair to follow Eli.

"You've got yourself a deal," Buck called after her.

When she entered Eli's office, she looked around at the masculine room. A lot could be learned about a person from the way they decorated their office. The furniture was the typically heavy leather and wood that men seemed to prefer and the mantel over the fireplace was decorated with pictures and sports trophies.

"I see you played football in high school," she commented.

"Yup. That's the reason I went to UCLA instead of the University of Wyoming," he said, closing the door behind them. "They gave me a full-ride scholarship to play for them."

"You must have been very good."

He shrugged. "I could hold my own."

Walking over to the fireplace, she took a closer look at the picture hanging above the mantel. It was a large photograph of a much-younger Buck and a woman holding a small boy.

"That's Buck and my mom with me on my fifth birthday," Eli said, coming to stand behind her. He wrapped his arms around her waist and pulled her back against his chest. "She was killed in a car accident on the way to Eagle Fork two weeks later."

"I'm so sorry for your loss, but I'm glad you got to know her," Tori said, wishing she could have known her mother. "Mine passed away when I was born and I have no memories of her at all."

His arms tightened around her in a comforting manner. "What about your dad?" he asked. "How long has it been since his death?"

She had told Eli that both of her parents were dead the first time he'd called to interview her. "My father died of a massive heart attack several months ago. He was under a lot of pressure and I guess it was too much for him."

She felt guilty for not telling Eli who her father was and why he had been under so much stress, but she wasn't sure she was ready for his reaction. What if he treated her like everyone else had when the story about her father was made public? People she had known all her life had suddenly looked at her with suspicion and intense loathing because her father had embezzled all or a sizable amount of their fortunes. The few who didn't looked at her with sympathy in their eyes. She wasn't sure which was worse—their hatred or their pity.

"I'm sorry, Tori," Eli said gently. "I'm sure you miss him a lot."

Turning in his arms, she stared up at him a moment before she shook her head. "I would love to be able to say that I do, but we were never close. He couldn't forgive me for causing my mother's death when I was born and the older I got, the more he seemed to despise me." She sighed heavily. "I'm told that I look just like her and I don't think he could come to terms with that."

Eli hugged her close as his hands moved over her back in a soothing manner. "I wish it could have been different for you, honey."

"Me, too," she said, wrapping her arms around his waist. "I wish my father and I could have had a relationship like you and Buck have. I know he drives you up the wall sometimes, but you love each other and there's nothing you wouldn't do for him or him for you. Treasure every moment of that."

When Eli leaned back to stare at her, the look in his dark brown gaze stole her breath. "Thanks for reminding me of how lucky I am, Tori. Yes, Buck can be hell to live with and I'd like nothing more than to throttle him at least a couple of times a day, but I've never spent a single minute of my thirty-four years doubting how much he cares for me."

Lowering his mouth to hers, Eli's firm lips moved over hers with such tenderness it brought tears to her eyes. The kiss was brief and more of an expression of understanding than passion, but it gave her hope that if they decided to make their marriage a real one, he might understand why she felt she had no choice but to keep her father's scandal concealed.

When he raised his head, he smiled. "How are your computer skills?"

"I can hold my own," she said, grinning as she returned his easy expression. "Why?"

Explaining that the breeding stock had all been tagged with a number, he added, "I have a new program designed to simplify my breeding records and give me a detailed analysis on each animal in a particular herd."

"In other words, you're looking for someone to input all of the data so you won't have to," she said, smiling.

His wide grin was unrepentant. "Yup."

"And what will you be doing while I'm slaving away with the data entry?" she asked.

He kissed the tip of her nose. "I'll be going over financial records and deciding whether or not to thin the herds or expand them, according to the latest market and futures reports."

"Running a ranch this size is like running a business," she said thoughtfully.

Having dealt with agricultural futures in her father's investment firm, she could have offered to help analyze the information. But she had left that life behind and she had no intention of ever doing that type of work again. She had only gone into financial planning as a way to get closer to her father. She'd mistakenly thought that if he saw she wanted to follow in his footsteps it might somehow redeem her in his eyes. Unfortunately, not even that made a difference in their relationship.

Eli led her over to his desk and booted up the breeding-record program for her. "I have everything you'll need right here," he said, handing her a stack of papers with columns of numbers and dates. After he explained which set of numbers identified the cows, the bulls they were bred to and the number of calves produced, he added, "I really appreciate this, Tori. It's going to save me a ton of time."

"I'm happy to do it," she said, seating herself in his desk chair.

While Eli sat in one of the big armchairs across the desk from her, going over the latest reports on cattle prices and the market projections, Tori entered the information into the computer. As she worked, she couldn't help but wonder if it would be like this if they decided to continue their marriage. It was comforting to think that if they did, they might work together to improve the ranch for theirs and the future generations of Laughlins.

"I don't know about you, but I could use a break," Eli said, stretching his arms. "What do you say we go see if Buck has lunch ready?"

"It's that time already?" Glancing at the clock, she couldn't believe they had been working for well over two hours.

He nodded as he placed the reports on the desk and got up to walk around behind the chair where she sat. His strong hands gently massaging her shoulders and neck felt like heaven.

"If you keep that up, I just might sleep through lunch," she said, closing her eyes. "Did anyone ever tell you that you have magic hands?"

His deep chuckle close to her ear seemed to vibrate all the way to her soul. "No, but if you think this feels good just wait until I—"

"If you two are ready, I got lunch on the table," Buck called from the other side of the closed office door.

"Be right there," Eli answered. Turning the chair away from the desk, he pulled her to her feet and into his arms. "Remind me later to tell you what else my hands are good at doing."

A mixture of awareness and anticipation streaked up her spine at the thought of his hands touching every inch of her body. They were getting closer to making their union real and she knew before that happened, she needed to tell him about herself and the reasons she answered his online ad.

But as they walked down the hall together, Tori wasn't sure how to approach the subject. What was she supposed to say—"Oh, by the way, I'm the daughter of the man who single-handedly created one of the biggest financial disasters since the Great Depression"? Or, "I'm responsible for turning my father in to the authorities when I discovered his nefarious business dealings"?

"I hope you've got big appetites," Buck said, grinning from ear to ear when they entered the kitchen.

"I don't know about Tori, but I do," Eli said, holding Tori's chair for her.

"My goodness, why didn't you come and get me to help you with all this?" she asked, clearly surprised at the amount of food on the table.

"It really wasn't all that much work," Buck said, shaking his head. "But I figured since I won't be around to fix supper tonight, I'd make a big lunch."

"Oh, that's right." Tori smiled at his father as she passed Eli a bowl of mashed potatoes. "I remember you saying you were planning on playing poker this evening."

Buck nodded. "Every Saturday night for the past five years."

Eli watched his father. He knew exactly what the old guy was up to. Buck knew the terms of the prenuptial agreement and he was hoping that by giving them time alone, they would make the decision to waive the get-acquainted period, consummate the marriage and stay together.

As he listened to Tori and his father chat about the

garden they were planning and where she should plant a few flowers, Eli thought about his wife and their unconventional union. He was having a hell of a time keeping his hands to himself and they were getting closer to doing exactly what Buck wanted. But Eli wasn't entirely sure it would be wise to make that kind of commitment just yet.

He hadn't heard anything from Sean Hartwell about the investigation. He had, however, reached the conclusion that he could overlook her misrepresenting her knowledge of farming and ranch work, as long as she had been truthful with him about everything else. Unfortunately, he wasn't sure how much longer he was going to be able to control his hormones when every last one of them demanded that he answer their call and make love to his wife.

"Eli, do you mind?" Tori asked, drawing him out of his disturbing introspection.

"What was that?" he asked.

"If I'm here in the spring, Buck offered to make flower boxes for the front porch so that I can plant flowers in them, and I wondered if that was something you would object to," she said, smiling.

He shook his head. "No, I don't have a problem with that at all."

As they continued to make plans, Eli decided he was going to have to talk to Buck and tell him that it might be a good idea to put any more projects on hold until a decision was made about Tori remaining on the ranch. There was no sense in looking forward to doing things that might not happen.

When the phone rang, he got up from the table. "I'll take that in my office."

Without waiting for Tori or Buck to respond, Eli walked down the hall to his office. Hopefully it was Sean reporting that other than her claim to have ranching experience, everything Tori had told him about herself was completely true.

Then he could give serious thought to taking their marriage to the next level and making love to his wife.

Six

"Has Buck already left for the poker game?"

Looking up from the computer, Tori nodded as she smiled at Eli. "He said not to expect him back until midmorning tomorrow. How were my girls?" He still wouldn't hear of her going out to feed the bucket babies and she missed the sweet little calves.

"They're doing just fine." He came over to where she sat behind the desk, and, turning the desk chair to face him, he propped his hands on the arms. Leaning down, he gave her a quick kiss. "What do you say to pizza in front of the fireplace in the family room for supper?"

"That sounds nice," she said, smiling. When she started to get up, he stopped her.

"Where do you think you're going?" he asked, pulling her up into his arms.

"I thought I'd go turn on the oven." She smiled. "That is a prerequisite to baking a pizza."

"Do you realize it's been a full day since I kissed you?" He shook his head. "That's just not right."

She frowned. "But you kissed me just now and earlier when we talked about my father."

"Those weren't real kisses," he said, grinning. "I'm talking about a 'down and dirty, make your knees weak and your head spin' kind of kiss."

"Oh, one of those," she said slowly. She had only seen the playful, teasing side of Eli a few times, but she really liked this side of him. She found it rather fun and very sexy. "What do you think we should do about that, Mr. Laughlin?"

"I've given it a lot of serious thought and I think I should kiss you." He leaned close to whisper in her ear, "It's the second-best way I know to get to know someone."

Her heart felt as if it stopped for a moment before beating double time. "What's the best way?"

"Making love." His heated look stole her breath and she couldn't think of a thing to say.

When his mouth came down on hers, Tori closed her eyes and savored the feel of Eli's lips nibbling at hers. He was quickly building a frustration in her that threatened her sanity. She suspected that he was doing it on purpose, too.

"Please, Eli…"

"Is something wrong, honey?" he asked as he continued to tease her.

"Please…kiss me," she said, wondering if that throaty female voice was really hers.

"I am," he said, sounding amused.

"No...I mean...really kiss me," she said, suddenly short of breath.

"You mean like this?" he asked a moment before he deepened the kiss.

Stars burst behind her closed eyelids as he used his tongue to explore her inner recess and stroke her with a tender, butterfly touch. If she had thought his kisses were powerful before, those had been mild compared to the one he was giving her at the moment.

Heat flowed through her veins like warm honey as he continued his sensual assault, and an interesting sensation began to build deep in the most feminine part of her. But when he moved his hand to cover her breast, the feeling became an almost-unbearable ache as he stroked her nipple through the layers of her clothing. Her knees suddenly seemed to be made of rubber as he continued to kiss her, and she grasped his shirt to keep from melting into a puddle at his feet.

"You want to know what I think?" he asked as he continued to tease the sensitive tip of her breast with his thumb.

He expected her to be able to speak after a kiss like that and with his hand still covering her breast?

Unable to find her voice, she simply nodded.

"As much fun as we're having right now, I think we should put this on hold while you bake a pizza and I build a fire." He kissed her forehead and, making sure she was steady on her feet, took her hand to lead her out of the office. "We'll reconvene in front of the fireplace in about thirty minutes to pick up where we left off."

Her legs felt wobbly as she went into the kitchen to

put a pizza in the oven and thought about his promise that they would be resuming the kiss. How much longer would they be able to hold out before the explosive chemistry between them took over and they made their marriage a real one? Was that what she wanted? She knew that she was starting to develop some very deep feelings for Eli. But was it love?

She'd never been in love before, so she had nothing to compare what she felt for Eli. If it wasn't love, it was close, and it wouldn't take a lot for her to fall head over heels for the man she had married.

But how did he feel about her? She knew he liked kissing her and she had felt the evidence of his desire each time he held her to him, but that didn't mean he was falling for her. As inexperienced as she was at lovemaking, she knew for a fact that a healthy, adult male didn't necessarily need an emotional connection with a woman to become aroused.

As she thought about her husband, she couldn't ignore the fact that they were close to throwing the month-long moratorium on the consummation of their marriage out the window. Before that happened and things got more complicated, she needed to tell him about herself and her reasons for answering his online ad. But she still hadn't been able to think of what to say to lead into it or how to break the news to him.

She knew Eli was a reasonable man, but would he understand her withholding the details of her background? How would he react when he learned about her changing her name, having all of her legal records altered to reflect that change and having the court records sealed to keep anyone from finding out who she really was? Would he understand just how guilty she felt for what her father had done to hundreds of innocent people?

Sighing, she removed the pizza from the oven. Before things went any further between them, she was going to have to confess. Husbands and wives shouldn't keep secrets of this magnitude from each other.

Tori only hoped that when she did talk to him about it, Eli would take her motivation into consideration and recognize that she'd had no other choice. Maybe then they could continue moving forward with their relationship and be free to make love without her feeling guilty about her deception.

While Eli finished building a fire in the stone fireplace, he thought about Sean's phone call. As of yet, the man hadn't been able to find anything, other than her claim to have experience with ranching, to indicate that Tori had lied about her background. He had gone on to say that at this stage of his investigation if something were terribly amiss, he usually had something concrete or at the very least a strong lead to follow. He did caution that nothing was conclusive and it might even take another week or so to conclude the investigation, but he wasn't anticipating much of anything turning up.

As Eli stared at the crackling flames, he told himself that it should only be a few more days and he would know for sure what decision to make. But his body was having a hell of a time listening to his mind and it had been that way since he'd watched her get off the plane in Cheyenne. And what happened yesterday sure hadn't helped matters. After seeing her luscious body when he'd stripped her out of her wet clothes, then lay with her in his bed as he shared his body heat with her, all he had been able to think about was making her his.

He took a deep breath. All he had to do was keep his hands to himself and not allow his hormones to cloud his judgment just a little longer. But it was going to be a true test of his fortitude. He could never remember wanting any other woman the way he wanted Tori. And knowing that it was perfectly acceptable for a man to make love to his wife wasn't helping, either.

"I hope you like pepperoni pizza," she said, walking into the room carrying a serving tray. "I wasn't sure what your choice of drink would be, but I took a chance on beer."

Turning to take the tray from her, he set it on the coffee table. "Good call, honey." He smiled. "Nothing beats having a beer with pizza."

Her sweet smile caused a warmth to spread throughout his chest. "I'm more of a cola kind of girl myself."

"Do you like mixed drinks?" If theirs had been a conventional relationship, it was something he would probably already know about her.

She shrugged. "I've had a few that aren't bad, but for the most part, I stick to soft drinks and iced tea."

He nodded. "And you drink coffee at breakfast."

"Doesn't everyone?" she asked, laughing.

For some reason, a streak of heat shot through him at the speed of light and it took every ounce of his willpower to keep from reaching for her. What the hell was wrong with him? He was in real trouble if something as simple as the sound of her laughter sent his libido into overdrive.

Deciding that sitting next to her on the couch might prove to be more than his self-control could handle, he asked, "Would you like to have a pizza picnic on the rug in front of the fireplace?"

She nodded. "I think that would be fun. I haven't been on a picnic in years."

"And it will be several more months before a picnic outside is possible," he said, lowering himself to the rug. Sitting face-to-face with a pizza between them should help him keep things in perspective and be a hell of a lot easier on his overtaxed willpower.

When they were settled on the colorful Native-American rug in front of the raised stone hearth, the glow from the fireplace bathed Tori in a golden light. She looked like an angel and Eli found it damned near impossible not to reach for her. With sudden clarity he realized it wouldn't matter where they sat or how far apart they were, as long as they were in the same room he was going to have a struggle keeping his hands off of her.

She placed a couple of pieces of pizza on a plate, and when she handed it to him their fingers touched and it felt as if a bolt of electric current shot straight up his arm. He took a big gulp of his beer and hoped that would cool the heat building within him. It didn't help.

Sweat popped out on his forehead and he almost groaned aloud when she licked a drop of pizza sauce from her finger. "Is something wrong with the pizza?" she asked when he continued to stare at her.

"No, I was just thinking that after we finish eating, I should probably go check on the mare and foal," he said, thinking quickly. Maybe a brisk walk in the cold night air would help clear his head and bring his traitorous body back under control.

"Is there a problem with them?" she asked, taking a sip of her cola.

"Not really," he said truthfully.

"Did you feed them earlier?"

"Yes."

"Then why do you need to check on them again?" she asked, looking puzzled.

He sighed heavily. He had never been, nor would he ever be, the type of man who took what he wanted from a woman without her being just as ready and willing as he was. But how was he supposed to tell her that all he could think about was making love to her until they both collapsed from exhaustion without frightening her? Hell, even he found the intensity of his need a bit unsettling.

"They should be fine," he finally admitted. He finished his pizza and the beer she had brought him without tasting any of it. "Would you like to watch a movie tonight?"

"Since we watched a romantic comedy the other night, I think we should watch something you're more interested in tonight." Her sweet smile sent his blood pressure off the chart. "Although, I would prefer one that isn't too scary."

"In other words, you don't want to lie awake listening for things that go bump in the night," he said, getting to his feet to retrieve the remote control.

While Tori carried what was left of the pizza back into the kitchen, Eli flipped through the movie channels, searching for an action-adventure film. Surely watching something with spies, car chases and a gun battle or two would be a safe bet for both of them. He could get interested in the storyline and it shouldn't be something that would keep her awake all night.

As he channel surfed for something suitable to watch, it bothered him that with each passing day he was thinking less about their marriage as a business arrangement and more about it becoming real. That wasn't supposed to have happened. At least not right away.

Oh, he had expected to develop a fondness for the woman he chose for his wife. But that was as far as he figured it would go. He also thought that it would be somewhere in the distant future and not to the degree that it clouded his judgment.

"When I looked out the kitchen window, I noticed that it's starting to snow again," she said, walking back into the family room.

Deciding to give it more thought while he was freezing his ass off under the spray of a cold shower, Eli settled himself on the couch. "Does the idea of more snow bother you?"

Was she getting tired of all the snow? Would she start complaining like his college girlfriend had done?

He almost hoped she did. It might put things back into perspective and help him get his priorities straight.

When Tori sat down beside him, she shook her head. "I love watching it snow. It's so pretty and peaceful."

Her enthusiastic expression was genuine and had him chastising himself for comparing her to his ex-girlfriend. They were nothing alike.

He put his arm around her and, drawing her close,

kissed the top of her head. "Maybe we can take the time to make a snowman tomorrow."

"Really? I've never made one before." She snuggled against him. "I would love doing that."

As the movie started, Eli glanced at the woman beside him. He liked doing things that made her happy, liked watching her wonderment at all of the new things she experienced. And he definitely liked the way she felt tucked to his side.

Damn! He was in real trouble.

Settling back against the couch, he tried to concentrate on the movie, but with Tori's sweet scent surrounding him and the warmth of her hand through his shirt where it rested on his chest, there wasn't a chance in hell that was going to happen. All he wanted to do— all he could think about—was kissing her again and a whole lot more.

Finally giving up, he threaded his fingers through her long, golden-brown hair and tilted her head up until their eyes met. "I'm going to kiss you until we both gasp for breath," he said. "Then I'm going to kiss you some more."

"I'd like that very much," she said, her violet gaze never wavering from his.

Without a thought to the consequences, he lowered his mouth to hers. He didn't want to think about how he would suffer through yet another cold shower or the sleepless night he faced lying in bed thinking about her being just down the hall. Nor did he want to analyze why he was willing to overlook her deception. Kissing her was quickly becoming as vital to him as the air he breathed and he couldn't have stopped himself if his life depended on it.

When her lips parted in a soft sigh, he slipped his tongue inside and, to his satisfaction, she leaned into him as if she wanted to be as close to him as he wanted to be to her. Stretching them out on the couch cushions, he pulled her on top of him and relished the feel of her delightful body aligned with his.

As he explored and teased her soft inner recesses, Eli could feel the tightening of her nipples against his chest through the layers of their clothing and his body's response was instantaneous. He was harder than hell and needed her more than he had ever needed anything in his entire life.

Breaking the kiss, Eli tried to remind himself of all the reasons that making love to her would be a bad idea. The investigation wasn't complete and they had a signed prenuptial agreement stating that they would wait a month to get to know each other before they consummated the marriage. At the moment, none of that mattered. All he wanted, all he could think about, was making Tori his in every sense of the word.

"I want you, Tori." He kissed his way along her jaw to the hollow behind her ear, drawing a whimpering moan from her. "I want to take you upstairs to my bed and spend the entire night getting to know you the way a husband knows his wife."

"I know it's...probably too soon...but I want...you, too," she said, sounding delightfully breathless. "But there's something I need to...tell you."

"What's that, honey?"

"I don't know what the protocol is for a situation like this, since I've never—"

"You've never made love before?" He wasn't sure he had heard her correctly.

She caught her lower lip between her teeth for a moment as she shook her head. "No, but that isn't—"

"You're a virgin?" Eli's heart stalled, then beat against his rib cage like a bass drum in a holiday parade.

"Yes."

A surge of heat flowed throughout his body and he had to take a deep breath to regain his control. No other man had ever touched his wife and Eli knew beyond a shadow of doubt that he wanted to be the one and only man to have that privilege.

Capturing her lips in a kiss that left them both gasping for some much-needed air, he stood up, then, taking her hands in his, pulled her up from the couch to stand in front of him. "Do you want to waive the moratorium and make this real between us, Tori?"

She looked a little dazed. "Y-yes."

There wasn't a moment's hesitation and it was all Eli needed to hear. Taking her by the hand, he started toward the stairs.

"We should probably discuss something first," she said, sounding a little hesitant.

"Do you want me to make love to you?" he asked as they climbed the steps.

"Yes, but—"

"I don't want you to worry, honey," he said, kissing her when they reached the top of the stairs. "We have all night and I promise to make sure you're ready for me." He kissed her again. "And if there's something else you think we need to talk about, it can wait until later. Right now, I'm going to make love to my wife."

His reassuring promise and the sound of his deep, sexy voice caused Tori's knees to wobble, and she forgot all about whatever she wanted to tell him. Nothing mattered but the man standing in front of her and what they were about to share.

As he led her down the hall to his room, her heart beat double time. She had waited her entire life for this man and this moment. Eli might be a millionaire, but he was honest, hardworking and had been more considerate of her than anyone she had ever known. She knew without question that she had fallen in love with him.

When he opened the door, led her over to the bed and turned on the bedside lamp, she realized that the promise he'd made the day before was about to come true. She was going to be lying in his bed with his arms around her and neither of them were going to be wearing clothes. The thought sent a wave of heat coursing through her so strong it threatened to swamp her.

"Tori, look at me."

Raising her gaze to meet his, the smoldering heat in Eli's dark brown eyes held such promise it stole her breath. "I don't want you to worry about protection," he said, his voice low and intimate. "I'll take care of everything."

"Thank you," she said, meaning it.

She hadn't given the matter a second thought. But as much as she would love to have a child, becoming pregnant right away might not be for the best. She wanted time for them as a couple, to nurture their relationship and enjoy each other for a little while before they started a family.

"I got to take your clothes off yesterday," he said, smiling as he caught her hands in his and brought them to the front of his shirt. "Your turn to take mine off me."

Tori knew Eli was allowing her to set the pace of their lovemaking, that he wanted her to feel completely comfortable with her decision to share her body with him. She loved him all the more for it.

As she unfastened each snap closure on his chambray shirt, she became more confident, and by the time she reached his belt buckle, she didn't hesitate to unbuckle the tooled-leather strap. When her fingers brushed his taut belly she heard his sharp intake of breath and glanced up. His eyes were closed and she couldn't help but rejoice in the fact that she instilled that degree of desire in the man she had come to care for so deeply.

Enjoying the feminine power coursing through her, she finished removing his shirt, then reached for the tail of his undershirt. As she raised it up and over his head, her eyes widened. Eli's chest was as beautifully sculpted as she'd imagined. His pectoral muscles were heavily padded, his nipples small round disks nestled in a thin cover of dark hair. Trailing her index finger down the shallow valley separating the rippling muscles of his abdomen, she stopped at his navel.

"Your body is beautiful, Eli." On impulse she leaned forward to press a kiss to his wide chest before tracing the line disappearing into the waistband of his jeans.

"I've been called a lot of things..." His deep laughter

sent intense longing to every part of her. "...but beautiful is a first for me, honey."

"It's true," she said, releasing the snap at the top of his fly. Noticing the bulge straining against the zipper, she caught her lower lip between her teeth for a moment. "Oh, heavens, I hope I don't..."

"Yeah, maybe I'd better take care of this," he said as he carefully lowered the metal tab. When he finished unzipping his fly, he smiled as he guided her hands back to his waist. "You're doing just fine. Feel free to continue."

As she slid the denim down his muscular thighs, she was glad that he had removed his boots when he'd come inside from feeding the bucket babies earlier in the evening. At least she wouldn't have to struggle with those, as well.

When he stepped out of his jeans and kicked them aside, her heart skipped a beat as she reached for the waistband of his boxer briefs. The evidence of his need was undeniable.

Concentrating on ridding him of the undergarment and his socks, she didn't look at him until they had joined the rest of his clothes on the floor. Then, taking a step back, she caught her breath. Eli was absolutely magnificent. The perfect specimen of a man in his prime. A very aroused man.

"We're even now," he said, taking her into his arms.

"I wasn't aware there was a competition," she said, smiling up at her handsome husband.

He shook his head. "There isn't. I just thought you'd be more comfortable if you weren't the first one out of your clothes this time."

"Thank you, Eli," she said, meaning it. "But I get the feeling you aren't the least bit intimidated about my seeing you naked."

"Nope," he said, pulling her sweater up and over her head. He tossed it on top of his clothes and reached for the front clasp of her bra. "The modesty gene isn't nearly as strong in men as it is in women."

That was apparent. He didn't seem the least bit concerned that he didn't have a stitch of clothing on, while she was quite self-conscious that he was about to see her completely nude for the second time. But when he brushed the straps of her lace bra from her shoulders, the look of appreciation in his dark eyes instantly erased all traces of her inhibitions.

"You're perfect," he said, cupping her breasts with his hands.

The feel of his calloused palms against her smoother skin sent a river of desire flowing straight to the most feminine part of her. But the touch of his lips as he kissed each hardened tip caused her to think that she might just go up in flames at any moment.

"Does that feel good, Tori?" His words vibrated against her nipple and sent a shock wave from the top of her head to the soles of her feet.

"Y-yes."

"The feelings are only going to get better," he said, reaching to unbutton the waistband of her jeans.

When he lowered the zipper, he slipped his hands inside the elastic band of her panties, then, skimming them along her hips and thighs, quickly slid the denim and lace down to her ankles. Stepping out of them, she braced her hands on his shoulders while he knelt to re-move her socks.

Rising to his feet, he took her into his arms. The feel of his body against hers and the hard ridge of his erection pressed into her lower belly caused her knees to give way.

He caught her to him, then swung her up into his arms. "Why don't we lay down?" he asked, placing her in the middle of his king-size bed.

When he stretched out beside her, he immediately pulled her into his arms and kissed her until light spar-kled behind her closed eyes. She loved Eli's kisses, loved that he made her feel things she had never felt before.

"We're going to take this slow," he said, nibbling kisses down to the slope of her breast. "I want you to trust me and feel completely comfortable with every-thing we do."

Before she had a chance to tell him that there was no one she trusted more, he captured her nipple with his lips and she couldn't have found her voice if she had tried. She was lost in the delicious sensations he was creating in every part of her body, and for the first time in her life she felt truly cherished.

As he continued his attention to her breasts a lazy heat began to flow through her veins and caused a tight-ening deep inside of her feminine core. But when he moved his hand down her abdomen to the apex of her thighs a shiver of nervous anticipation ran the length of her.

"Part your legs for me, Tori," he whispered against her skin.

Closing her eyes, she did as he commanded and when he gently touched the most sensitive part of her, a tingling excitement streaked straight up her spine. He stroked her with a featherlight touch and she felt as if she would melt from the exquisite sensations he created.

Tori felt an emptiness deep inside of her that she knew in her heart only Eli could fill. She needed him to make her feel whole. She needed to feel as if she was a part of him.

"Please...Eli," she said, unable to verbalize what she wanted.

"Do you want me, honey?"

"Y-yes."

He slipped his finger inside of her and she thought she would surely be reduced to a cinder as a wave of pleasure so strong she had to remind herself to breathe washed over her. Lost in the delicious feelings flowing through her, it took a moment for her to realize that Eli had rolled away from her to retrieve a foil packet from the bedside table.

"This probably isn't going to be as pleasurable this first time as it will be later on," he said, kissing her with such tenderness it brought tears to her eyes. "But I promise to make this as easy for you as I possibly can."

Nudging her legs farther apart with his knee, he held her gaze with his as he guided himself to her. Slowly, carefully, Tori felt his body push into hers, and she held her breath.

"Try to breathe normally, honey," he said, his voice sounding strained. "It will be more uncomfortable if you're tense."

When she concentrated on relaxing her body, he gave

her a smile that warmed her all the way to her soul as he lowered his head to cover her mouth with his. Lost in his kiss when he pushed past the barrier, Tori realized that it hadn't hurt the way she had anticipated.

"Are you okay?" he asked, raising up on his elbows.

"Yes," she said, realizing it was true.

A fine sheen of perspiration covered his forehead and she knew the toll his restraint was taking on him. He was giving her time to adjust and she loved him all the more for it.

"Tori, I need to love you now," he said, gently drawing the lower part of his body back, then pushing himself forward.

As he set a slow pace, she marveled at the feeling of truly being one with the man holding her. She had never felt more connected emotionally with anyone in her entire twenty-six years as she did with Eli.

But all too soon, the delightful sensations he created within her began to change into an urgent need and she instinctively knew she was close to the culmination they both sought. Eli must have sensed her need for release because as he thrust into her, he moved his hand between them to touch her intimately. Tiny feminine muscles immediately tightened deep inside of her a moment before pleasure rippled throughout her entire being.

As Tori slowly floated back to reality, she felt Eli go perfectly still a moment before he surged into her a final time and she knew he'd found his own relief from the passionate tension that had held them captive. Reluctant to end the bonding of their bodies, she held him close when he collapsed on top of her.

If she'd had any doubts, they had just been erased. She wasn't sure how it could have happened so quickly, but she had fallen hopelessly in love with Eli.

Seven

"I'm too heavy for you, honey," Eli said, levering himself away from Tori. When he moved to her side, he gathered her to him. "Are you all right? I didn't hurt you, did I?"

"Not at all," she said, shaking her head. "And you were right about what you told me this morning in your office."

"What's that?" He wasn't sure how it was possible so soon after making love to her, but her smile caused the blood in his veins to surge and he felt himself becoming aroused all over again.

"Your hands really are magical." He wasn't sure if the rosy glow on her cheeks was the remnant of passion or a touch of embarrassment. Either way, she'd never looked prettier to him.

"Now that I can think a little more clearly," he said, grinning, "could I ask you something?"

She nodded. "I suppose you're wondering why I'm so inexperienced."

"Yup." He kissed the top of her head. "Don't get me wrong. There's no way in hell that you'll ever hear me complain about being the only man you've made love with. But by the time most women reach their mid-twenties, they've lost their virginity."

"I can't really say I was dedicated to waiting for my husband or that I didn't come close a couple of times," she said, snuggling closer to his side. "It just never felt like it was the right time or I was with the right man until now."

Even though it would probably be considered his due as her husband to make love to her, Eli couldn't help but feel privileged that Tori had waited for him. It not only supported her claim to have high moral standards, it told him that she considered him to be the right man for her.

The thought was so arousing, he had to dig deep for the strength to resist making love to her again. But that wasn't an option at the moment. She had never made love before and although he had managed to make her first time a pleasurable experience, her body had to be tender from the newness of it all, and he didn't want to run the risk of making her sore.

"Are we going to make love again?" she asked.

She must have felt his reaction. When she looked at him, Eli could see the blush of desire on her cheeks and knew as surely as the sun rose in the east each morning that she wanted him again as much as he wanted her.

"No. As much as I would like to, we won't make love again until tomorrow." He would pay a high price for his nobility, but he refused to cause her any more discomfort than he already had. "You're new to this and you need a little time to adjust."

"Okay," she said, sounding a little disappointed as she laid her head on his chest and snuggled close to his side. "I am a bit tired." Within a moment or two, he heard a slight change in her breathing and knew she had fallen asleep.

Reaching over, Eli turned off the bedside lamp and closed his eyes. But sleep eluded him. He couldn't stop thinking about the woman with her head pillowed on his shoulder.

The final report from the investigation would only take a few more days. Why hadn't he been able to wait to make their marriage real until he had heard that everything was fine with Tori's background?

The preliminary word indicated there was nothing to worry about and that's what he'd concentrated on. He took a deep breath. He should have been thinking with his head, not his hormones.

When they'd both agreed to waive the rest of the get-acquainted period, it had greatly upped the stakes. Instead of ten thousand dollars and a quick annulment if things didn't work out between them, Tori would get a million dollars and he would end up with a very expensive set of divorce papers.

But he didn't think that was going to be the case. Surely a woman who waited all this time for the right man to make love to her wouldn't share that part of herself if she wasn't completely committed to the marriage. Besides, he trusted her. She'd lied once, but now that they were together, he didn't believe she'd keep anything else from him.

Deciding the die had been cast and there really wasn't anything he could do now, Eli forced himself to relax. Only time would tell if he was the luckiest man on the planet to have advertised for a wife and ended up finding the woman of his dreams. And he didn't want to spend any more time dwelling on the other possibility.

"How are my girls this morning?" Tori asked as she entered the spacious enclosure where the two orphaned calves were kept.

At the sound of her voice the two calves trotted over to vie for her attention. She knew they were only wanting their breakfast of milk replacer and grain starter, but she didn't care. Daisy and Buttercup had become her adopted babies and she loved spending time with them.

While the calves devoured their meals, Tori thought about her evening alone with Eli. She had become Eli's wife in every sense of the word and nothing would ever make her regret that. But making love with him had greatly complicated their situation.

She had tried to tell him that she had something they needed to discuss before they made love. But he hadn't been interested in listening and she had been so caught up in the moment, she had quickly forgotten why it was so important to tell him about her past before they took the next step in their unusual relationship.

Sighing, she stared off into space. Eli had been so considerate, so caring, last night—surely a man with that kind of compassion would listen and be able to understand why she had made the decision to keep her identity hidden. Now all she had to do was find the right time and way to tell him.

"It looks like you and the bucket babies are getting along pretty well," Eli said from behind her.

Glancing over her shoulder, she smiled. "Checking up on us?"

He shook his head as he let himself into the enclosure. "After I took care of the mare and foal, I thought I'd see if you want to build a snowman with me."

"Really?" He had mentioned building one the other night, but she wasn't sure he remembered it.

His smile warmed her through and through as he nodded. "Yup." He put his arms around her. "By the way—Buck called and it looks like the poker game has turned into a marathon. He said he won't be back until late this evening or tomorrow morning."

"Is that unusual?" she asked, enjoying the feel of his arms around her.

"Not really." Eli gave her a quick kiss. "But this time, I think he's making an excuse to give us some more time alone."

Her cheeks heated. "He knows that we... Oh, dear heavens."

"No, he doesn't know anything," Eli said, grinning. "But he's been hoping we'd make this arrangement permanent and I'm sure he thinks by giving us time alone, we'll come to that conclusion."

She felt a little better. When Buck did return from spending time at the bunkhouse on the other side of the valley, his room was downstairs and on the opposite side of the house from the master bedroom upstairs. At least they would have that privacy.

"Are you doing okay?" he whispered close to her ear. "You aren't too sore, are you?"

Wrapping her arms around his waist, Tori rested her head against his broad chest. How could she not love a man so concerned for her comfort and well-being?

"Other than waking up alone, I'm fine." She leaned back to look up at him. "Why didn't you wake me to help out with the chores?"

He kissed the tip of her nose. "I thought I'd let you sleep in."

"Thanks to you, I'm fully recovered from my dip in the icy pond," she said, frowning.

He smiled as he used his gloved finger to brush a strand of hair from her cheek. "That's not why I wanted you to get your rest."

"Then why—"

"I plan on keeping you up tonight making love," he said, his voice low and intimate.

"Oh." She buried her head in his chest. "Forget that I asked."

"Do you have any idea how cute you are when you get embarrassed?" he asked, his rich laughter making her feel warm all over.

"No, and a gentleman wouldn't call attention to it," she said, shaking her head.

"Honey, I'm as much of a gentleman as the next guy," he said, kissing the side of her neck. "But there's no need to be embarrassed with me. I'm the man who explored all of your secret places last night and I intend to do so again tonight." His candidness caused her heart to skip a beat. "Now, if you're finished here, let's go wash up the buckets and get ready to build the best snowman you'll ever see."

More comfortable with the change of topic, she nodded. "I'll see you two girls this evening."

"Actually, I wanted to talk to you about that," Eli said, opening the gate to let them out of the enclosure. "With Buck staying over at the bunkhouse, I thought you might make supper for us while I feed the calves."

Tori caught her lower lip between her teeth as they rinsed out the bucket she had used for the milk replacer. Heating up a pizza was one thing, but making dinner was something else entirely. Especially when she had grown up with a family cook and the culinary skills she'd acquired lately only extended as far as the directions on the back of a package.

"That sounds fine," she said, deciding that it couldn't be that hard to tear up a salad, put a couple of steaks on the built-in stovetop grill and bake a couple of potatoes in the microwave.

"Now let's go build your first snowman," Eli said when he returned from storing the buckets in the feed room.

As they walked the distance to the house, Tori dismissed her concerns over making dinner. If she ran into any problems, she could always consult one of Buck's cookbooks or use Eli's computer to do an internet search.

"What do we do first?" she asked when they reached the front of the log home.

"Make a snowball and then roll it along, packing the snow around it as you go," he said, bending down to get a handful of white fluff. "We're lucky last night's snow wasn't as dry as it is most of the time."

"That makes a difference?" she asked, doing as he instructed.

He nodded. "Dry snow is like powder and better for skiers, but wet snow packs tight and makes a better snowman."

In no time the ball she had started with was a large sphere of packed snow. "Do I make one slightly smaller for the middle?"

"Yup, then I'll lift it up on top of this one while you make one even smaller for the head," he said, flattening the top of the ball she had just made.

When they had the three sections in place, Tori stood back to survey their effort. "This is fun, but there's a lot of work that goes into making a snowman, isn't there?"

Nodding, Eli handed her a handful of dark rocks. "Push these into the head for his eyes and mouth while I go raid the refrigerator for a carrot."

When he returned with the carrot, he held a couple of sticks, an old cowboy hat and a battered leather vest. "I thought you might like to give him an outfit," he said, smiling.

"I think it's only fitting that we make him a snow cowboy," she agreed, laughing. Adding the finishing touches, Tori stood back to look at her first snowman. "I think this is the best snowman…cowboy ever."

"Stand beside him," Eli said, taking his cell phone from his pocket. He clicked off several pictures of her with the snowman, then started toward the house. "Now that we have the pictures for posterity, let's go inside and see what we can rustle up for lunch."

"Not before I do something I've wanted to be able to do all my life," she said, shaking her head as she bent down to pick up a handful of snow.

Packing it into a tight ball, she lobbed it at his broad back. It hit dead center, leaving a dusting of snow on his shearling coat.

"Oh, no. You did not just do that," he said, laughing. He bent down to get a handful of snow in one smooth motion as he turned to face her. His evil grin promised retribution. "This will not go unchallenged, honey."

Laughing, she took off, but running through the knee-high snow was like moving in slow motion. "Sorry!" she called over her shoulder.

"No, you're not," he said at the same time a blast of snow hit the middle of her back.

Realizing she was no match for his long throws and accuracy, she fell on her stomach into a snowdrift. Quickly grabbing a handful of snow, she waited for Eli to come over to see about her.

"Tori?"

She remained silent and perfectly still as she waited.

"Honey, are you all right? I swear I didn't think I threw the snowball that hard." Was that a hint of panic in his voice?

When Eli knelt down beside her and turned her face up, she smiled as she smeared the handful of snow across his lean cheek. "You didn't throw it *that* hard."

"So it's going to be like that, is it?" he asked, grinning as he wiped the snow from his face with his gloved hand.

The teasing promise of revenge in his dark brown eyes quickly had her wishing she had given more thought to what she would do for a quick getaway. Lying prone on the soft snow with Eli hovering over her, she was trapped.

If she could distract him, she might get away with it. Reaching up to put her arms around his neck, she pressed her mouth to his. As she moved her lips over his, a surge of feminine power flowed through her when he groaned and caught her to him. Encouraged by his response, she used her tongue to coax him to open for her, and, slipping inside, she teased and stroked him as he had done her so many times over the past week.

"I think you're going to send me into orbit," he said, easing away from the kiss. He sounded as out of breath as she felt. Getting to his feet, he pulled her up from the snowdrift and held her to him. "Let's go inside, warm up and have some lunch."

"That sounds good," she said, loving the way he held her to his side as they walked toward the back porch. He was apparently going to overlook her rubbing snow in his face.

"Then after lunch we'll discuss how I intend to get even with you for making me think I hurt you," he said, opening the door for her.

She glanced up at his handsome face and saw that if the look in his eyes was any indication, the payback he had in mind was going to be extremely enjoyable for both of them. "Would it help make amends if I said I was sorry and kissed you again?" she asked with a smile.

"Probably not," he said, laughing. He gave her a quick kiss. "But that doesn't mean it wouldn't be a lot of fun for both of us if you tried."

* * *

"I think it's time for me to go take care of the calves," Eli said, stretching.

After lunch they had gone into his office to work on inputting the information into the new breeding-records program and it had taken the entire afternoon to get it finished. But it would have taken him twice as long if not for Tori. She had been a tremendous help and he could envision them working together to make the Rusty Spur even bigger and better for future generations of Laughlins.

"I suppose I should start making supper," she said, rising from the desk chair. "How does a steak, baked potato and salad sound?"

"Honey, you're talking to a cattle rancher," he said, putting his arm around her shoulders as they walked down the hall toward the kitchen. "It sounds like the perfect meal."

"How would you like your steak?" she asked, going to open the refrigerator while he pulled on his boots.

"Medium, but I rarely get it that way," he said, shrugging into his coat. "Buck thinks that if you toss it in a pan and brown both sides, that's good enough."

"Isn't that a bit undercooked?" she asked, frowning.

"Not for Buck." Eli laughed. "He likes his steaks rare and has no problem telling anyone who will listen that as long as the horns are lopped off and it doesn't moo anymore, it's cooked just right."

"Remind me to cook my own from now on," she said, placing two steaks on the stove's built-in grill.

As he walked out to the barn to feed the bucket babies, Eli looked forward to getting the chore finished so he could get back into the house with Tori. He still hadn't evened the score with her for the face full of snow and making him think he had hurt her when he'd hit her with the snowball.

Grinning, he thought about ways to make her pay. Every one of the scenarios he came up with ended in them making love.

As he scratched the back of one of the calves, Eli wondered if he would have to keep them close to the house until after Tori had their first child as Buck said he'd had to do with Eli's mother. Just the thought of Tori growing round with his child, watching his baby nursing at her breast, sent a shaft of heat streaking through his veins at the speed of light.

He took a deep breath to ease the sudden tension gripping his lower body. When had he started thinking about pregnant women being sexy? The thought alone was reason enough for him to question his sanity.

But as he gave it more thought, he realized it wouldn't be just any pregnant woman he would find desirable. Only Tori.

Eli shook his head. How had he gotten in so deep, so fast? They had only been married a week, and they had made love only once.

None of that seemed to matter. He wanted Tori with a hunger that was staggering, wanted to have babies with her and spend the rest of their lives making the Rusty Spur Ranch the biggest and best it could be.

He frowned as he let himself out of the enclosure to wash the buckets and store them in the feed room. Had he fallen for her?

Shaking his head, it was all he could do to keep from

laughing out loud at his own foolishness. Love hadn't been and wasn't going to be a factor in his decisions regarding their marriage. There was no doubt that he was fond of Tori and that he desired her, but when he'd set out to find a wife, he had been determined to keep emotions out of the equation. It was the only way he could be objective about what was best for the ranch. Just because they had made love didn't mean that had changed. Starting a physical relationship with Tori just meant that they had made more progress toward their arrangement becoming permanent.

Satisfied that he had his perspective firmly in place, he walked back to the house. "Do you need help finishing up supper?" he asked, entering the kitchen.

"No, I think I have everything under control," she said, glancing up from the two small bowls of salad she had just finished tearing up. "While you wash up, I'll set the table."

He nodded as he went down the hall to wash his hands in the downstairs bathroom. The thick, ominous odor of something burnt hung in the air like a bad omen and Eli couldn't help but wonder if he would have to wait until he went down to Eagle Fork in the spring to get a good steak.

"I'm not sure, but I think the steaks may be just past the medium stage," she said, setting his plate in front of him.

Glancing down at the charred piece of beef on his plate, Eli was certain that in biblical times it would be considered a burnt offering. But one look at the hopeful expression on Tori's pretty face and he knew as surely as he knew his own name, he was going to eat the damned thing and tell her it was the best steak he'd ever had.

"It looks good," he lied. He just hoped Buck had a stash of antacids somewhere in the first-aid cabinet in the pantry. He had a feeling he was going to need them.

As they ate, they talked about his strategy for the breeding program and her plans for a garden, and by the time the meal was finished, Eli decided that he would talk to Buck about teaching her how to cook. Many more meals like the one he had just consumed and he was certain he would have to seek medical attention for the treatment of an ulcer.

"How would you like to spend the evening in front of the fireplace again?" he asked.

"That sounds nice." She rose from the table to rinse their plates and put them in the dishwasher. "When I was looking for potatoes to bake for supper, I found some marshmallows and graham crackers in the pantry."

"There should be some chocolate bars around here somewhere," Eli said, leaving the table to walk up behind her. He wrapped his arms around her waist and pulled her back against him. "Buck developed a sweet tooth in his old age and always keeps them on hand."

"Making s'mores sounds like fun," she said, turning in his arms to face him. "I've only had them once, when I was in Campfire Friends, and that was years ago."

"I'll bet you looked cute in your uniform," he said, thinking about how she would look now in a pair of shorts and a formfitting camp shirt. His body tightened predictably and he had to shift to relieve the pressure in his suddenly too-snug jeans.

"The troop never got around to ordering uniforms because it disbanded almost as soon as it was formed," she said, oblivious to his dilemma. "After a night in the troop leader's backyard, most of the kids decided that outdoor activities weren't for them."

"Were you one of those kids?" he asked, hoping she wasn't.

"Not at all." She shook her head. "I was really looking forward to going on a camping trip somewhere, but that never happened."

"I'll take you camping," he promised. Grinning, he added, "There's nothing like sleeping outdoors, especially if the sleeping bag is designed for two."

"That sounds interesting. Do you have one of those?" she asked.

He laughed. "No, but you can damned well bet I will by the time we go camping."

"You're incorrigible." Her smile indicated that she didn't mind at all.

"Nope, I'm just a man who's looking forward to getting cozy under the stars with his woman." The thought caused his body to tighten further, and he had to force himself to move away from her. "I think if we intend to spend a little time in front of the fireplace, I'd better find the roasting forks for the marshmallows and build a fire in the fireplace while you find Buck's chocolate bars."

A half hour later, Eli sat on the plush rug in front of the crackling fire in the stone fireplace, watching Tori lick the sticky marshmallow residue from her fingers. It was all he could do to keep from groaning.

"This was a nice idea," she said, smiling.

"When we go camping up in the mountains this summer, they'll taste even better," he said, leaning over to kiss away a small drop of melted chocolate at the corner of her perfect lips. "There's something about sitting around a campfire on a mountaintop that seems to enhance everything."

"Everything?"

He nodded as he pulled her into his arms. "Kisses are sweeter, and when we make love under the stars they'll seem so close that you'll feel like we're a part of them."

"I do believe you're a romantic, Mr. Laughlin," she said, kissing his chin.

"Just wait and see," he said as he stretched them out on the rug in front of the hearth.

Lowering his mouth to hers, Eli quickly forgot about anything but the woman in his arms. She tasted of chocolate and marshmallow and he didn't think he had ever savored anything quite so erotic or sexy.

"I've tried to do the right thing and not make love to you too soon after taking your virginity," he said, kissing his way to the hollow at the base of her throat. "But I want you more than I want my next breath, Tori."

"I want you, too," she said, staring up at him with a light of desire in her violet eyes that caused his mouth to go dry. "Please make love to me, Eli."

Eight

There was a sultry tone to Tori's voice that caused Eli's body to harden so fast it left him feeling light-headed. Without a word, he helped her sit up, then pulled her sweatshirt over her head and tossed it onto the couch. Quickly removing her bra, he cupped her breasts and lowered his head to kiss each tightened tip.

"I'm going to love every inch of you and when I'm finished, I'm going to start all over again," he said, taking one of her nipples into his mouth.

When she moaned and threaded her fingers through his hair to hold him to her, Eli knew she was as turned on as he was. He paid homage to first one of her breasts, then the other, and when he lifted his head, he loved the blush of passion on her creamy cheeks. She didn't need just any man—she needed him.

The thought sent a surge of heat to his groin and,

taking hold of the lapels of his chambray shirt, he unfastened the snap closures with one quick jerk of his hands. Pulling his undershirt off, he sent both garments to join her sweatshirt and bra on the couch.

Tori immediately placed her hands on his chest and the feel of her soft palms caressing his skin made the temperature in the room go up a good ten degrees. Closing his eyes, he reveled in the fact that she was as fascinated with his body as he was with hers. But when she pressed her lips to one of his flat nipples, Eli felt as if his head might fly right off his shoulders.

"I think we'd better slow this down, honey," he said, feeling as if the oxygen had been sucked out of the room.

"I love touching you," she said, giving him a smile that reached his soul.

"Let's get the rest of these clothes off," he said, wanting to feel her hands on other parts of his heated body, as well. "Then you can touch me all you want."

Helping her out of her slacks and panties, he quickly shucked his jeans and underwear. Then, laying her back on the rug, he knelt beside her. The flames in the fireplace cast a golden glow over her alabaster skin and he knew for certain he had never seen a more beautiful sight. As he stared down at her perfection, he noticed she seemed just as enthralled with his body.

"You make me want you in more ways than I ever thought possible," he admitted as he stretched out beside her, cradling her in his arms.

"And I want you just as much," she said, running her delicate hand along his side.

He could tell she wanted to touch him but was unsure if she should. Catching her hand in his, he kissed her fingertips. "Part of making love is exploring and learning more about each other."

Facing each other, her eyes never left his as she moved her hand over his hip and beyond. When she found him, Eli ground his back teeth and held his breath as he struggled for control. Her featherlight touch on his heated body was heaven and hell rolled into one as she tested his strength and weight.

"I think we'd better put the discovery phase on hold for a while, honey," he said, taking her hands in his. He took several deep breaths in an effort to regain control. "Otherwise, I'm going to be embarrassed and you're going to be extremely disappointed."

"Please make love to me, Eli." The desire in her eyes and the passion in her voice convinced him that her need was as great as his.

Moving to sit up, he reached into the pocket of his discarded jeans. After arranging their protection, he lifted her to straddle his thighs. "Put your legs around me," he said as he eased her down onto him.

Her eyes widened as her body consumed his. "Oh, wow!"

"Are you okay?" he asked, feeling a moment of apprehension.

She nodded as she circled his neck with her arms and rested her head against his shoulder. "I'm fine. I just feel...so...complete."

He remained perfectly still as he gave her time to adjust and gave himself a moment to savor her tight body surrounding his. But the feel of her intimately holding him and her budded nipples pressed to his chest proved too much for him to resist. He needed to complete the act of loving her or go completely insane.

When he guided her into a gentle, rocking motion, he knew she was feeling the same passionate lure he was when her head fell back and a tiny moan escaped her lips. His focus began to narrow, and he realized that he was close to finding his release. But he was determined to ensure her pleasure before his own.

Kissing the column of her neck and the slopes of her breasts, he deepened his strokes and in no time he felt Tori begin to tighten around him. She was close to reaching her climax and, quickening his pace, Eli felt her body begin to rhythmically caress him as she found her fulfillment. Only then did he let go of his restraint and give in to his own satisfaction.

As they continued to hold each other, Eli knew if he hadn't already fallen for the woman in his arms, he didn't have far to go. She was everything he had ever wanted in a woman.

Having Tori at the ranch had been good for all concerned and, although it made him nervous as hell to admit it, he couldn't imagine life on the Rusty Spur without her. He enjoyed the time they spent working together doing chores and setting up the new system for the ranch records. And lately, he had noticed there was a little more spring in Buck's step. Since his retirement, Eli hadn't seen his father as excited about anything as he was about the garden he and Tori were going to plant in the spring. Buck even seemed to have mellowed a little and wasn't quite as cantankerous as he had been in past years.

Tori might have a few secrets that she hadn't divulged when he'd interviewed her, but he seriously doubted they would amount to much. Besides, who didn't have a few things in their past they'd rather forget? He hadn't told her about his college girlfriend, and the scam she had tried to pull off. If he hadn't wised up when he did, he would have lost a lot more than his pride. He would have lost a sizable chunk of the Rusty Spur, as well as the Laughlin fortune.

But Tori was nothing like the barracuda his former girlfriend had turned out to be. It was past time for him to stop looking for her to slip up and accept that Buck's assessment of her was right on the money. Tori was a good person and there was no reason to continue looking for something in her background that wasn't there. He'd call Sean tomorrow and call off the investigation.

When he leaned back to look at her, he smiled. "You're amazing, Tori."

"I was thinking the same thing about you," she said, nodding. "That was incredible."

Lifting her off his lap, Eli reached for a couple of throw pillows and the plush throw from the couch. Then, lying down, he pulled her back against him and covered them both with the throw.

They were quiet for some time, and Eli liked that they were content just to be with each other. But as he stared at the crackling flames in the fireplace, something kept bothering him. Tori had given him her best over the past week and he hadn't really done anything nice for her in return. She had done chores around the ranch practically from the moment she'd arrived, cut his deskwork time in half and kept his father off his back by planning a garden for the spring.

And what had he done for her in return to show his gratitude? Treat her to a night in front of the television? Help her build a snowman and put her in danger of freezing to death by letting her ride a horse he knew full good and well she didn't know how to control? Hell, he hadn't even let her plan her own wedding. He was the one who'd made all of the arrangements for their brief marriage ceremony.

A slow smile began to tug at the corners of his mouth. That was the one thing he *could* do something about. He could give her the wedding of her dreams.

With his mind made up on what he intended to do for Tori, he relaxed and felt himself start to drift off to sleep. "Let's go upstairs to bed, honey."

"There's something we need to talk about," she said as he stood up and helped her to her feet. "I wanted to tell you last night, but—"

He yawned. "Sorry. What were you saying?"

"Never mind. You can barely hold your eyes open," she said, shaking her head. "We can talk tomorrow when we're both more awake."

As they gathered their clothes and walked upstairs to his bedroom, Eli decided that Tori wasn't the only one with something to discuss. He had something he wanted to talk over with her, as well.

Under the circumstances, as weddings went, theirs had been a rushed affair with little celebration, and she deserved better. He needed to tell her to start planning the wedding of her dreams, and this coming summer, they would invite the whole damned state to witness the renewal of their vows.

* * *

The next morning when she entered the kitchen, Tori found Buck whistling a tune as he made breakfast. "You must have won some money at the poker game," she said, smiling.

"Good morning, Tori-gal," he said, grinning as he reached for a cup and poured her some coffee. "No, I actually lost a couple of hundred dollars."

"And you're happy about it?" she asked, taking the mug of coffee he handed her.

"Easy come, easy go." He shrugged. "Sometimes I win, sometimes I don't. It's just the nature of the game."

"I suppose that's one way of looking at it," she said, setting her cup down at her place at the table. "Is there something I can help you with?"

"Nope, I think I've got everything just about ready." He frowned. "Where's Eli?"

"He's taking his shower."

"No, I'm finished," Eli said, walking up behind her. He surprised her when he put his arms around her, then kissed the side of her neck. "What's for breakfast, Buck? I'm starved."

Until that moment, Eli had refrained from showing her much affection in front of Buck. That he did so now sent a clear message to his father that they intended to make their marriage permanent.

She watched a twinkle of approval in Buck's dark eyes as he looked from her to Eli. "I've got the usual," he said, his grin wide. "Just have a seat, and I'll get it dished up for you."

Tori's chest swelled with emotion when she realized that she had finally found the place where she belonged. For the first time in her life, she felt that she was part of a family and it felt absolutely wonderful. Buck treated her like a daughter, the way she always wished her father had done. And although Eli hadn't told her how he felt, she knew he had feelings for her. It was enough for now. In time, maybe he would even come to love her the way she loved him.

It bothered her that she still hadn't found the right way or the opportunity to tell him about her past. Eli deserved to know everything and she wanted to tell him. But last night when she realized how tired he was, she knew that it wasn't the right time. But today, she was determined to rectify that. Before they proceeded with their relationship, she needed to tell him whom he had married and she hoped with all of her heart that he would understand why she had handled things the way she had.

With her mind made up, she listened to Eli and Buck talk about what they had planned for the day and couldn't keep from smiling. Their relationship had improved greatly over the past week and she enjoyed seeing them more relaxed around each other.

Remembering Grandma Jean's words the day they were married—that it wasn't right that Buck refused to attend the ceremony—Tori realized that she had been the source of the tension between them. Buck had probably objected to Eli finding a wife on the internet and as outspoken as the older man was, had no doubt told Eli so. But being as stubborn and independent as his father, Eli had defied Buck and asked her to join him on the Rusty Spur. She didn't have a clue what she had done to change Buck's mind, but he seemed perfectly content with her and Eli's arrangement now and that was all that mattered.

"What do you want me to do today, besides feeding Daisy and Buttercup?" she asked.

"Now that all of the men are fully recovered from the flu, there's really no reason for you to be out in the cold," Eli said as he finished his breakfast. "After you take care of the bucket babies this morning, why don't you come back to the house and help Buck make lunch?"

"In other words, you want him to teach me how to cook," she said, laughing. Her steak the night before had been just as charred as his, and she knew Eli had only eaten it to keep from hurting her feelings.

"Honey, you bake a great frozen pizza," he said, grinning. "But as steaks go, there's room for improvement."

Rising from the table, she took her plate and his to the sink to rinse them. "It was pretty bad, wasn't it?"

"Don't worry—you'll get better at it," he said, walking over to put his cup in the dishwasher. Lowering his head, he gave her a kiss that curled her toes. "I've got some things to take care of this morning, but I'll see you at lunch."

After Eli put on his coat and hat and left the house, Tori's cheeks heated when she turned to find Buck staring at her with a wide grin. "Looks like we'd better start makin' some concrete plans for that garden and your flower boxes," he said happily.

Just as Eli reached the horse barn to check on the mare and her foal, the phone rang in the feed room.

What did Buck want now? he wondered as he picked up the receiver. He had just told his father his plans for the day not fifteen minutes earlier.

"Sean Hartwell just called and wants you to call him back as soon as you can," Buck said when Eli answered. "He told me to tell you it was real important."

Eli's heart stalled then began thumping against his ribs as if he had run a marathon. "Thanks. I'll give him a call as soon as I feed the mare and foal."

"What the hell is he callin' about this early in the mornin'?" Buck demanded.

Eli closed his eyes as he tried to hang on to his patience. He wasn't as irritated by Buck's question as he was nervous that Sean had found out something about Tori. He understood more than ever the meaning behind the saying "Don't shoot the messenger" because at the moment, that was exactly what he felt like doing. Dead men couldn't tell tales and everything could go on as they had been for the past week.

"I had him check on something for me," Eli answered his father.

"Dammit, son, you had Tori investigated, didn't you?" The anger in Buck's voice was undeniable.

"Yes." Before his father could start in with a tirade about knowing Tori had good reason for whatever she'd done, Eli added, "We'll talk about this later, Buck."

As he hung up and started scooping oats into a bucket, Eli knew in his heart he wasn't going to like what Sean had to say. Why else would the man have insisted on Eli calling him right back if he didn't have bad news to report about Tori's background? He couldn't think of a single positive reason for Sean to be calling him at six in the morning. By the time he finished taking care of the mare and her baby, Eli wasn't any more ready for his upcoming conversation with Sean, but he couldn't put it off any longer. It was time to find out what the investigation had turned up. Then he could decide how to proceed.

Picking up the phone, he dialed Sean's number. "Sean, Eli Laughlin here. What did you find out?"

"You're never going to guess who you married," the man said. Was that a touch of disbelief he heard in Sean's voice?

"Why don't we dispense with the guessing games and you just come right out and tell me?" Eli asked, angered by the fact that Sean had found anything at all in Tori's background.

"You married Victoria Bardwell." Sean paused as if waiting for Eli to digest that bit of information before he continued. "She's the only child of John Bardwell, the single most hated man in the history of the financial industry. And up until he was arrested, she worked as a financial planner at the Bardwell Investments Agency."

"I think you're mistaken," Eli insisted, clinging to the hope that the man was wrong, but knowing deep down that he wasn't. "My wife's maiden name is Anderson."

"She had her name legally changed after her father died of a massive heart attack five months ago. I checked with one of the people who wrote her a letter of reference—" he heard the sound of Sean shuffling papers "—a judge by the name of Byron Stiers, and everything checked out fine. But I hadn't been able to find her other reference until yesterday evening when I tracked her down in a nursing home just north of Charlotte. Marie Gentry is recovering from a stroke and has some short-term memory loss, but her long-term memory is quite clear. She was Victoria's nanny and told me all about your wife's mother dying when she was born and how Victoria had spent her life doing everything she could to win her father's approval."

A knot the size of his fist twisted at Eli's gut. When he'd talked to Marie, she hadn't told him any of that. She hadn't been in a nursing home, either. She'd probably had the stroke after he'd talked with her about Tori.

"Did you find out anything else?"

"Yeah," Sean said hesitantly. "When she left Charlotte, Victoria was dead broke and close to being homeless after her condo and car were sold to help pay some of her father's clients."

A throbbing began to pound at his temples and Eli felt like the biggest fool ever to walk on two legs. "Is that it?"

"There are a couple of other things I'm going to check out, now that I have her real name," Sean said. "But I thought you would want to know about this as soon as possible."

"Yeah. Thanks."

When he hung up the phone, the knot in Eli's gut began to turn into a burning ball of outrage. How could he have been so damned stupid? Why had he let his guard down, knowing from the day they'd met that Tori was hiding something?

He had let his desire for her get in the way of his good sense, and even with the prenuptial agreement, the cost of his mistake was higher than he could have

ever imagined. The money he would owe her when she
left the ranch didn't matter to him. It paled in compari-
son to the price he was going to pay when she walked
away with his heart.

As she finished feeding Daisy and Buttercup, Tori
thought about the past week and how everything had
worked out. Now there wasn't a doubt in her mind that
she had done the right thing by accepting Eli's offer
of marriage. She'd found the home and family she had
always wanted and a man that she loved with all of
her heart.

Hopefully her happiness would be complete once
she told him who she really was.

Sighing, she absently scratched the calves' backs as
she stared off into space. Husbands and wives should
be aware of each other's secrets and especially one the
magnitude of hers. She only hoped that he would understand and realize that the only thing she had lied to
him about was her knowledge of the rural way of life.

"Tori, we need to talk." Eli's voice brought her out
of her disturbing introspection and back to the present.

Smiling, she turned to find him standing a few feet
away. He looked furious.

"Is something wrong?" she asked, opening the gate
to the calves' enclosure.

"We'll talk when we get to the house," he said, his
voice tight.

What could have happened in such a short amount
of time to alter his mood so drastically?

Tori practically had to jog to keep up with his long
strides in the newly falling snow. When they entered

the house, she barely managed to get her coat removed and hung on one of the pegs before Eli took hold of her elbow.

"Don't disturb us," he ordered as he hurried her past Buck on the way to his office.

Had he discovered her secret? Was that why he was so angry?

She couldn't imagine how that was possible. When she'd sought legal counsel about changing her name for reasons of protection, she had been assured that her true identity would be kept completely confidential. She had even been issued a birth certificate, driver's license and social security number under her new name, and the court records had been sealed to ensure her privacy. Unless she told them, no one was supposed to know who she really was.

"Have a seat," Eli said, pointing to one of the armchairs in front of his desk.

Fear clawed at her insides as she shook her head. "I don't think—"

"Sit," he commanded. Although he hadn't raised his voice, there was a steely edge in his tone that warned her he wasn't in the mood to be defied.

"What is this about, Eli?" she asked as she perched on the edge of the plush leather chair. It was easier than arguing, and she wasn't sure her shaky legs would support her.

She had a sick feeling in the pit of her stomach that her worst fears were about to be realized. Eli had somehow found out who she was before she could tell him.

"Were you ever going to tell me that I had married a fraud?" he asked pointedly. "Or were you going to let me believe you were everything you seemed to be right up until you decided to move on to greener pastures?"

"I—I'm not a fraud," she said, shaking her head. It felt as if her world were crashing down around her and there didn't seem to be any way to stop it. "And I did try to tell you who I was before we made love the first time, and then again last night."

"You should have tried a little harder." He clearly didn't believe her.

"I had my name legally changed to Victoria Anderson because I had to," she said, hoping he would allow her to finish her explanation.

"I'm sure you did," he said, his tone cutting. "The Bardwell name has become one of the most recognized in the country because of your father's embezzling from his clients' accounts. You wouldn't have been able to carry out your own scam if you'd gone by your real name."

"No, that isn't it at all." She had to get him to listen to her. "I had nothing to do with his illegal activities."

"You're telling me that you worked for him and didn't know what was going on?" His emotionless smile chilled her all the way to the bone. "I'm not buying it, Tori."

"I honestly didn't know what he was up to until just before it all began to unravel." Tears began to spill down her cheeks, but she impatiently wiped them away with the back of her hand. Her heart felt as if it were shattering into a million pieces. "I was the one who—"

"Save it," he said, jerking open one of the drawers in his desk to pull out a checkbook. When he began to fill it out, he added, "I'd rather not hear you try to justify your actions. You obviously decided to hide out here for a while until things cooled down and you could move on to something bigger and more lucrative." He tore off one of the checks and shoved it across the desk at her. "But I suppose you made out well enough. By making sure we consummated the marriage, you get a nice cool million with your divorce papers, instead of the ten thousand you would have gotten for an annulment."

A cold like nothing she had ever known spread throughout her body. "Keep your money," she said, rising to leave. His mind was made up about her and there wasn't anything she could say or do that was going to change it. It was the same as when her friends found out about her father. The same as when anyone heard her last name. Eli was no different. "I don't want it."

"Take it," he insisted, coming around the desk to stuff it into her hand. "There's a flight back to Charlotte this evening. I want you packed and ready to leave by this afternoon."

"Didn't our lovemaking mean anything to you?" she asked as tears streamed unchecked down her cheeks. "How can you so easily forget what we shared? How can you forget about us?"

"Oh, I remember what we shared, but I don't think we have the same perception of what it meant." He shook his head. "I should have known better than to let desire get in the way of what's best for the ranch."

"Was desire all that you think it was, Eli?"

He stared at her for several long moments before he finally nodded. "What else would it be?" Before she could answer, he motioned toward the door. "Now, if you'll get your things together, I'll see that someone takes you to catch your flight to Charlotte."

He wasn't even going to take her to the airport himself?

Straightening her shoulders, she sniffed back a fresh wave of tears. She might be penniless and once again alone in the world, but she had her pride.

"I'm not going back to Charlotte," she said, tossing the crumpled check onto his desk. "There's nothing left for me there."

"Where will you go?"

"That's really no longer any of your concern, now is it?" she asked, knowing that he really didn't care as long as it was nowhere near the Rusty Spur Ranch.

He shrugged. "I just need to know where to ship your things."

"I'll let you know when I get there," she said, walking to the door. Turning back she added, "And if I don't get back to you, feel free to dispose of them however you see fit."

As Tori folded the clothes she intended to take with her, she had to stop frequently to wipe the tears from her eyes. How could everything have fallen apart so fast?

This morning she had awakened in the arms of the man she loved more than life itself and within a few hours he had essentially told her he never wanted to see her again. He wouldn't even listen to her tell her side of what happened and why she had taken the measures she had to obliterate Victoria Bardwell in order to become Tori Anderson.

She briefly wondered how Eli had discovered her secret. But it really didn't matter. He had found out and as hard as it was to face, he had tried and found her guilty before he'd even bothered to confront her about it.

But what upset her more than anything was the fact that they had decided to make their marriage a real one, and at the first sign of a problem, he was ready to give up. The least he could have done was acted like a real husband and sat down with her to try to work out their problem. But he had his mind made up and wouldn't listen to anything she said.

A knock caused her heart to skip a beat until she heard Buck quietly say her name. "Tori-gal?"

Walking over to open the door, one look at the older man with his arms spread wide to gather her to him, and she dissolved into a torrent of tears. She had not only lost the man she loved, she had lost her newfound family.

"There, there, gal," Buck said, moving them over to sit on the side of the bed. Patting her on the back as she sobbed against his shoulder, he added, "It's going to be all right."

Shaking her head, she leaned back to look at the man she had come to think of as her adopted father. "Eli wants me to leave, Buck."

"He told me," Buck said, nodding. "But don't worry. You're not going anywhere for a while."

"Buck, that's sweet of you, but I can't stay where I'm not wanted," she said, wiping at her eyes. "I've had to live that way most of my life and I can't do it anymore."

"I can't fault you for feelin' that way," he said, his eyes filled with understanding. "But you can't leave now because the snow we've been gettin' all mornin' has turned into a blizzard. And once it stops, we won't be able to get out of the valley until the men can fire up one of the tractors and blade the road over the ridge to the main highway. That'll take several more days."

Her heart sank. She couldn't think of anything more uncomfortable or heartbreaking than being stranded with the man she loved when all he wanted was to have her out of his life for good.

"This is terrible, Buck," she said, rising from the bed to go over and look out the window. Snow was falling so hard and the wind gusts were so strong, she couldn't even see the barns. "Does Eli know?"

Buck shrugged. "Hard to tell. He's been holed up in the office with the door closed for the past hour."

"He won't be happy about this," she said, feeling more miserable by the second. She wasn't sure what would be worse—having him send her away or having to stay with him and see the contempt in his eyes.

"Give him a little time to cool down," Buck advised. "Right now, he's about as friendly as a pissed-off wolverine. He won't listen to anybody, and it's best we leave him alone for a spell."

"I doubt he would give me the chance even when he does calm down," she said, shaking her head. She wasn't sure how much Eli had told Buck about her, but it no longer mattered. "He doesn't want to hear about my father or the reason I had to change my name and leave Charlotte."

Buck held up his hand to stop her. "I don't know anything about it and, as far as I'm concerned, it doesn't matter. I know that you did whatever you felt you had to do." He smiled as he rose from the side of the bed to leave. "Eli's the one you need to talk to first. Then, if you want to tell me, I'll listen. And if you don't, it won't change my opinion of you."

Long after Buck left to go back downstairs, Tori stared out the window at the falling snow. The older man's feelings for her were unconditional. He had decided that she was a good person and that whatever she'd done wouldn't change his opinion or make him feel differently about her. Why couldn't his son give her that same consideration?

Deciding there were no answers, she returned to the dresser to remove her clothes and continue packing. At least when the snow finally did let up, she would be ready to leave as soon as someone could drive her out of the valley. Then she would purchase a ticket to wherever her meager funds could take her.

Sitting in the dark, Eli poured himself another shot of whiskey as he stared out the window at the moon rising over the new-fallen snow. The winter blizzard had moved on a couple of hours ago, but he hadn't felt the need to leave the sanctuary of his office. If he did, he might run into Tori and that was something he wanted to avoid. He didn't need to be reminded that he had fallen yet again for a deceptive woman with an agenda to make a fool of him.

At least he'd caught on to his college girlfriend before he'd got in over his head. She had tried her damnedest to get him to partner with her "brother" and develop part of the Rusty Spur into a resort or dude ranch. At the time, he'd been so enamored of her that he had considered trying to talk Buck into making the man a partner in the ranch.

Eli shook his head and muttered a guttural curse. He could still remember the disillusionment and betrayal he'd felt when he'd discovered that the "brother" she had been so fond of was actually her fiancé and that they were con artists. Had he not taken a step back after she'd visited the ranch, he might not have realized that things weren't the way they seemed, until it was too late.

But Tori had gone above and beyond with her scam. She had changed her name and married a complete stranger in order to get ahead.

He had thought he had all the bases covered this time around. He had done a fairly thorough background check on her, spoken with the authors of her letters of reference, and as far as he could tell they were on the up-and-up. Then he'd had an iron-clad prenuptial agreement drawn up to protect his assets before he married her.

The only thing he hadn't counted on was being fool enough to fall for her and not having the willpower to keep his hands to himself long enough for Sean to complete his investigation.

"So much for your foolproof plan, Laughlin," he muttered as he downed the whiskey, then poured himself another shot.

Given his track record, he would probably do well to swear off women altogether and make provisions in his will to leave the Rusty Spur to the state for a park or wildlife habitat. Doing that was probably his best option. Just about anything was preferable to the hell he was going through now after learning the truth about Tori.

Tossing back the shot, he rose to his feet to go upstairs to bed. There wasn't enough whiskey in the world to numb the pain of falling hard and fast for a woman, only to learn she was just as nefarious as the rest of her gender.

Nine

Two days after the blizzard, Tori was stir-crazy. She'd stayed in the bedroom she had used since her arrival and even waited to go downstairs for her meals and out to visit the calves until she was certain Eli had gone outside to help his men with some of the other chores.

She had asked Buck about the road and when he thought the men would get around to using the tractor to clear the snow, but he had just shrugged and told her they would get around to it eventually. It wasn't that she was so anxious to leave the Rusty Spur. She wasn't. But the longer she stayed, the harder it would be for her when the time came for her to go.

"Tori, could you come downstairs?" Buck called. "I need your help with something."

She frowned as she walked out of her room and descended the stairs. It wasn't like Buck to yell up the stairs for her. If he had wanted to talk to her or needed her help with something over the past couple of days, he'd climbed the stairs and knocked on her door.

"What can I help you with, Buck?" she asked when she entered the kitchen.

Buck was standing at the sink, and when he turned around she gasped at the sight of the bloody towel he had wrapped around his hand. "I was cutting up some steaks for a stew and the butcher knife slipped," he said, clearly disgusted with himself. "It cut my finger."

"How bad is it?" she asked, hurrying over to him.

"I'm gonna need a few stitches," he said, holding his finger under the water to rinse the wound. "You'd better run and get Eli."

"But the road isn't cleared for him to take you to the doctor," she said, rushing into the pantry to get the first-aid kit she had seen on one of the shelves.

"He'll have to stitch it up for me," Buck said, using the hydrogen peroxide she'd removed from the box of medical supplies.

"Where is he?" she asked, reaching for her coat. Seeing Eli again wasn't going to be easy, but Buck needed help that she couldn't give.

"Try the equipment barn," he said. "Eli said something at breakfast about needing to do work on one of the trucks."

Running through the snow, she went straight to the barn Buck had mentioned. She found Eli working on the truck he had taught her to drive the day she'd helped him take hay out to the pasture.

"Buck cut his finger," she said when he looked up. "He needs you to stitch it closed."

Nodding, he wiped his hands on a rag. "Go back to the house and have him hold it above his heart and apply direct pressure on it to help stop the bleeding. I'll be right there."

Eli looked so good to her that she thought she might burst into tears. She loved him so much that she ached from it, but he wasn't willing to listen to her and she wasn't going to grovel.

When she got back to the house, Buck sat at the table holding his finger up and it appeared he was applying pressure to the wound. "Eli's on the way," she said, hanging up her coat and removing her snow boots. "Has the bleeding slowed down?"

Buck nodded. "But it looks like you're gonna have to cook supper tonight."

Sitting down at the table beside him, she shook her head. "You heard what a disaster it was when I tried to grill steaks."

"Don't worry—I'll talk you through it," he said, smiling. "You'll do just fine."

When Eli entered the house, took off his coat and washed his hands, he walked over to where Buck sat at the table with Tori. "Let's see what you've done this time."

"What does it look like?" Buck snapped back. "I had a run-in with the butcher knife and lost."

"That's because you aren't careful enough when you use it," Eli shot back.

Their sniping at each other continued the entire time Eli was sewing up Buck's finger and Tori didn't like it one bit. The tension between them was even worse now than it had been the day she'd arrived at the ranch. And she knew she was the cause of their problem, again. Buck was clearly on her side and thought Eli should listen to her explanation and Eli was too stubborn to hear anything she had to say. But she couldn't stand the thought that she was the reason for the deterioration of their relationship.

"Stop it, both of you," she said suddenly, surprising even herself at her outburst. But once she started, she couldn't seem to stop herself. "You're the only family either of you have and no matter what your differences are, you care deeply for each other. So start acting like it." She pointed at Eli. "You have something that I've never had—a father who loves you and wants the best for you. Believe me, not every father cares enough to want that for their child. You should cherish your relationship and show some respect for him."

Turning to Buck, she added, "And you need to stop antagonizing your son because he doesn't want me to be his wife anymore. I love him, but he doesn't love me. You're going to have to accept that things didn't work out between us, and move on. Once I leave the ranch, I'll be out of your lives, but you'll still have each other. Take care of what you have together and never take it for granted or lose sight of how precious it is."

Clearly rendered speechless by her uncharacteristic outburst, both men stared at her as if she had sprouted another head.

Deciding that she had said more than enough, she turned and left the room to go back upstairs. Why did men have to make something as simple as love so darned complicated? And why was it breaking her heart that she wouldn't be around to remind them each and every day what a special bond they had?

As Eli watched Tori storm from the room, he looked at Buck. His father was just as startled by Tori's lecture as he was.

"I guess she told us how the bread's buttered," Buck finally said.

Eli nodded. "She certainly had no problem sharing her opinion on the subject."

They were both silent while Eli wrapped gauze around Buck's finger, then secured it with tape.

"Family sure does mean a lot to her," Buck said, his voice suspiciously gruff. He cleared his throat. "It reminds me of the way your momma always felt."

"She lied to me, Dad," Eli said, putting the medical supplies back into the first-aid kit. "How could I ever trust her?"

"Maybe you ought to hear her out before you decide one way or the other," his father suggested. "She might have a pretty good reason for doing what she did."

"I don't see how she could ever justify lying to me about who she is," Eli answered as he closed the first-aid kit.

"Other than telling you she had ranchin' experience, what else did she lie about?" Buck asked.

Eli frowned. "I'm not sure. She wasn't honest about her name, but she wasn't exactly dishonest, either."

Buck looked confused. "You wanna run that past me one more time?"

"She had her name legally changed, so technically

when she told me her name was Victoria Anderson, she was telling the truth," Eli said slowly.

Now that he had calmed down a little and given himself a couple of days to think about it, he had to concede that omitting the facts wasn't the same as lying. But it wasn't exactly being honest, either.

Buck seemed to ponder the information. "Well, as I see it, if you don't give her a chance to tell her side of things, you'll never know what the whole story is."

Eli shrugged. "I don't guess it would hurt."

"No, it wouldn't." Buck pointed toward the upstairs. "That little gal up there is your wife, son. Be a husband and go talk to her. Find out what she has to say before you go throwin' away somethin' that you might never find again."

Returning the first-aid kit to the shelf in the pantry, Eli hesitated for a moment. He was half-afraid her explanation wouldn't be plausible. But if her reasons were solid and he let her leave without hearing what they were, he would lose the only woman he had ever truly loved.

He sucked in a sharp breath. When had he fallen in love with her? And how could he have abandoned his resolve to keep emotions out of their marriage?

He wasn't sure how all that had happened. But he did know as surely as he knew his own name that if he didn't listen to Tori, he'd never know whether he was protecting himself and the ranch or throwing away the best thing that had ever happened to him.

"Will you be all right for a while?" he asked Buck.

His father nodded. "I'm just gonna sit here and look through my seed catalog." His father gave him a smile that reminded Eli just how lucky he really was. "Good luck, son."

"Thanks, Dad."

As Eli climbed the stairs, he wondered what he was going to say to Tori. Should he tell her he was ready to listen to her explanation? Or should he ask her why she hadn't trusted him with her secrets when things had started getting more serious between them? Or maybe he should tell her about his college girlfriend and how her duplicity had left him with a few trust issues of his own.

Knocking on the bedroom door, Eli waited for a moment before he opened it. Tori was sitting on the window seat, staring down at the snowman they had made a few days ago.

"Tori, I think we need to talk," he said, walking over to sit down beside her. He winced when she drew her legs up and wrapped her arms around her knees, pressing herself into the corner away from him.

"Why?" she asked, sniffing. She had been crying and it caused a knot to form in his gut that he was responsible for her tears.

He stared across the room at the packed suitcase. "There's something I should probably tell you about myself that might explain why I wasn't willing to listen to you."

"Why should I listen to you when you wouldn't listen to me?" she asked, still staring out the window.

"Because you're more reasonable than I am?"

"I'm glad you finally realized that," she answered.

They were silent for several long moments before he cleared his throat. "When I was in college, I dated a girl and I thought we were pretty serious," he said, deciding to tell her everything. "But it turned out she and her fiancé had a plan to swindle me and Buck out of whatever they could get."

"Her fiancé?" Tori finally turned to look at him. "She was engaged and dating you, too?"

He nodded. "She told me he was her brother and that he was a land developer who was interested in building a resort or possibly a dude ranch somewhere in Wyoming. She tried to get me to partner up with him and put his name on the deed to part of the ranch. Had I fallen for their scheme I would have probably ended up losing at least part of the ranch and if not all of our money, a sizable amount of it."

Tori frowned. "How did you get hooked up with these people?"

"I met up with her when I attended UCLA," he said, thinking about how naive he had been at the time. "I didn't know it, but they had researched my family and would have shown up at whatever college I attended."

"They targeted you," Tori guessed.

"Yup. They knew my family had land and money and they decided to go after some of it." He shrugged. "To make a long story short, I figured out that things weren't right when I brought her here for Thanksgiving. She hated the place and couldn't seem to stop calling her 'brother.'"

"So because of her, I've been condemned for the painful decisions I was forced to make," Tori said defensively.

"Unfortunately, that just about sizes it up," he said, taking a deep breath. He wasn't proud of his condemnation of her without listening to her, but he was man enough not to try denying it. "If you're willing and still want to tell me, I'm ready to listen. So, why did you need to wipe the slate clean and start over as another person? And why did you go so long without telling me, even after we made love?"

"Before I tell you what happened, I'd like to know how you discovered who I really am," she said, meeting his gaze head-on.

"I hired Blake Hartwell's brother, Sean. He's a retired FBI agent and owns his own investigation agency. He was just about to close his investigation when he found your former nanny. She told him all about you."

"How could Nanny Marie betray me like that?" she asked, her voice cracking.

Eli shook his head. "In her defense, Sean said she's had a stroke and it's affected her short-term memory. She might not remember even writing that letter of reference or having that conversation with me."

She sighed. "I hope she'll be all right. She's the closest thing to a mother that I've ever known and I think she really did want what's best for me. She even encouraged me when I told her my plans to change my identity."

"I know who your father was and that you weren't close, but why did you feel that changing your identity was the only answer?" he asked, hoping she had a reasonable explanation.

"After the reaction you had, you have to ask?" She rose from the window seat to pace the room. "What were some of the first words out of your mouth when you confronted me the other day?" Before he could answer, she told him. "You said you had a hard time believing that I worked for my father and had no knowledge of his illegal activities. You decided I was as guilty as he had been just because of the Bardwell name."

The more he thought about it, Eli felt as guilty as hell. That was exactly what he had done.

"Yes, I discovered what my father was doing with his clients' accounts," she went on. "And I did become involved, but not in the way you think."

"I'm listening," he said, sensing that what she was about to tell him was crucial.

"After I learned what he had been doing, I confronted him and told him that he needed to turn himself into the authorities or I would." Tears began to spill down her cheeks and she wrapped her arms around her middle protectively. "He refused and told me to do what I felt I had to do."

"You turned him in," Eli said, knowing that must have been the hardest thing she'd ever had to do.

She nodded. "Even though I knew it would kill any chance of us ever having a relationship, I didn't feel I had a choice. He had stolen billions of dollars from his clients and I couldn't ignore that. That's why I met with the authorities and gave them the information to bring it to an end. I was promised that the name of the whistle-blower would remain anonymous."

"But it wasn't?" He could tell she was still haunted by the decision she'd been forced to make.

"It was, but he knew and…so did I," she said, her breath catching on a sob. "When he had the heart attack from the stress of his arrest and the charges he was facing, I was called to the hospital, but he refused to see me."

Eli didn't think twice about going to her and wrapping her in his arms. "Honey, I am so sorry you had to go through that."

"I wish that's all I had to go through," she said, sounding drained of energy.

"What else happened?" She had been through hell and he should be horsewhipped for putting her through more by not letting her explain the first time she'd tried.

"Even though I had been cleared by the authorities of any involvement, no one would hire me because of my last name. And because everything I owned was tied to my father's business, I lost my condo, my car and all but a few mementos the authorities decided weren't worth trying to sell off to repay the people he stole from." She snuggled deeper into his embrace. "After I received a couple of death threats from some of his understandably furious clients, I petitioned the court to have my identity changed for reasons of protection."

The thought that she might have been hurt or worse was almost more than he could bear. "But how did you find my online ad? And why did you feel compelled to answer it?"

"I ran across it by accident while researching areas of the country where I could make a fresh start on the least amount of money." She leaned back to look up at him. "I have no explanation other than fate as to how I found your ad or why I felt I had to answer it."

Staring down at her, he smiled. "Did you mean it when you said you love me?"

She hesitated a moment before she finally nodded. "Yes. But I realize you don't love me."

"That's where you're wrong, Tori," he said, knowing that he wanted nothing but complete honesty and trust between them. "I love you more than life itself."

He had tried to deny it, but he was pretty sure he had fallen in love with her the first time he had talked to her on the phone. Why else would he have based his decision to ask her to marry him on the sound of her voice?

"Can you find it in your heart to forgive me for all of the accusations? And for my stubborn refusal to listen to you?" he asked, praying that she could.

Her tearful smile was without a doubt the prettiest he had ever seen. "Yes. But I was at fault, too."

"How do you figure that, honey?" he asked, happy to have her back in his arms.

"I should have found a way to tell you about myself when I realized how quickly we were getting close to making our marriage real." She stared up at him. "And I should have told you the truth about not knowing how to ride. If I hadn't lied about my experience with rural life, the accident would have never happened."

"We were both to blame, Tori."

Covering her mouth with his, he tried to kiss away the hurt he'd put her through and any lingering doubt she might have that he loved her. When he finally eased away from the kiss, they were both short of breath.

"Will you do me the honor of staying married to me, honey?" he asked, needing to know she wanted to be his wife for the rest of their lives as much as he wanted to be her husband.

"Yes." There was no hesitation in her answer and

her beautiful smile convinced him that he had to be the luckiest son of a gun to ever draw a breath if she still loved him in spite of his stubborn pride.

"Then I want you to start planning the wedding of your dreams," he said, grinning. "And don't tell me you don't already have something in mind. From what I hear, most girls start planning their weddings in kindergarten."

She laughed, and he didn't think he'd ever heard a sweeter sound. "Now that you mention it, I might have had an idea or two about my wedding when I was that age," she admitted.

"Set a date for some time this coming summer, honey," he said, unable to stop grinning. "I love you and I damned well want everyone to know it."

"And I love you, Eli Laughlin, with all my heart and soul."

Epilogue

Lying in her husband's arms after making love, Tori stared up at the endless night sky. It was filled with more stars than anyone could ever count and most of them looked as if they were so close she could reach out and touch them.

"You were right," she said, kissing Eli's bare shoulder.

"About what, honey?" he asked, caressing her inside the sleeping bag made for two.

"Up here on the mountain, it really does feel like we were making love among the stars." She smiled as she watched a shooting star streak across the heavens. "I'm glad you decided this is where we should spend our honeymoon."

"It was something I wanted you to see," he said, cupping her breast.

"I thought your dad looked very nice in his tux this afternoon," she said, loving that Buck had been more than happy to walk her down the aisle.

"I think that Grandma Jean thought so, too," Eli said, laughing. Blake Hartwell's grandmother had not only attended the wedding, she had taken it upon herself to be the unofficial wedding coordinator, as well as Buck's unofficial date for the celebration.

As they lay in each other's arms, gazing up at the most amazing sky Tori had ever seen, she smiled. She had one more secret that she had kept from Eli for the past two weeks and it was time she let him know what it was.

"We should talk," she said, running her hand over his wide chest.

His thumb teasing her nipple stilled. "I'm listening."

"Remember you telling me that you wanted to take me on a Caribbean cruise for our first anniversary?" she asked, moving her palm down to his stomach.

"Yup. I thought you might like to go somewhere warm in the dead of winter." His voice sounded a bit strained and she knew he was becoming aroused again.

Turning to her stomach, she placed her forearms across his chest, resting her chin on the backs of her hands. "I think I have somewhere else in mind that we should go sometime during the last week of January."

"Where's that, honey?" he asked, giving her a smile that sent her temperature soaring. "Tell me where you want to go and I'll make sure to take you there."

"I think we'll probably need to spend some time at the hospital in Cheyenne," she said, loving him more than she ever dreamed possible.

He frowned. "You want to tell me why?"

"Because that's when our baby is due and I—"

"Baby?" He sat up in the sleeping bag and pulled her up with him. "You're pregnant?"

Nodding, she kissed him soundly. "I've known for a couple of weeks, but I wanted to wait and give you the news as my wedding gift to you."

"Honey, you couldn't have given me a better present." The love she saw in the depths of his dark brown eyes stole her breath.

"Buck is going to be beside himself," she said, laughing. "I think he started hinting that he would like a grandchild right after we started planning our vows renewal."

Eli grinned. "He'll spoil the poor kid rotten."

As he lay back in the sleeping bag and pulled her down on top of him, Tori had never felt more loved or happier.

She was finally realizing her life's dream. She was the wife of the man she loved with every fiber of her being and there was no doubt in her mind that he loved her just as much. She was finally part of a real family and she was going to have a baby she could love and nurture. And all because she'd taken a chance and answered an ad to find love in a rancher's arms.

* * * * *

"No Messena bride would wear anything but these jewels."

"There must be something smaller, cheaper in the box—"

"If there was, no Messena bride would wear it," he repeated.

The words *Messena bride* sent a small thrill through her. "I'm not a bride—not even close."

"And that's not even close to an excuse." Picking up her left hand, Gabriel slipped the ring on the third finger.

She blinked, unexpectedly emotional, because the ring, this scene, was something she had never dared dream about. Yet here she was, and Gabriel had just placed the most beautiful engagement ring she had ever seen on her finger. It should have meant fidelity and undying love—instead it was all a charade.